shield maiden

by

richard denning

Shield Maiden
Written by Richard Denning
Copyright 2012 Richard Denning.
First Published 2012.
ISBN: 978-0-9568103-7-3
Published by Mercia Books

A catalogue record for this book is available from the British Library

Book Jacket design and layout by Cathy Helms
www.avalongraphics.org

Copy-editing and proof reading by Jo Field.
jo.field3@btinternet.com

Graphics and map by Gillian Pearce
http://www.hellionsart.com/

Author website:
www.richarddenning.co.uk

Publisher website:
www.merciabooks.co.uk

Anglo Saxons Runes are Germanic Font 2 from:
http://www.fontspace.com/dan-smiths-fantasy-fonts/anglosaxon-
runes with permission from Dan Smith

ᚠᛟᚱ ᛗᚨᛏᛏᚺᛖᚹ
For Matthew

The Author

Richard Denning was born in Ilkeston in Derbyshire and lives in Sutton Coldfield in the West Midlands, where he works as a General Practitioner.

He is married and has two children. He has always been fascinated by historical settings as well as horror and fantasy. Other than writing, his main interests are games of all types. He is the designer of a board game based on the Great Fire of London.

Author website:
http://www.richarddenning.co.uk

Also by the author
Northern Crown Series
(Historical fiction)
1.The Amber Treasure
2.Child of Loki

Hourglass Institute Series
(Young Adult Science Fiction)

1.Tomorrow's Guardian
2. Yesterday's Treasures

The Praesidium Series
(Historical Fantasy)
The Last Seal

The Nine Worlds Series
(Children's Historical Fantasy)
Shield Maiden

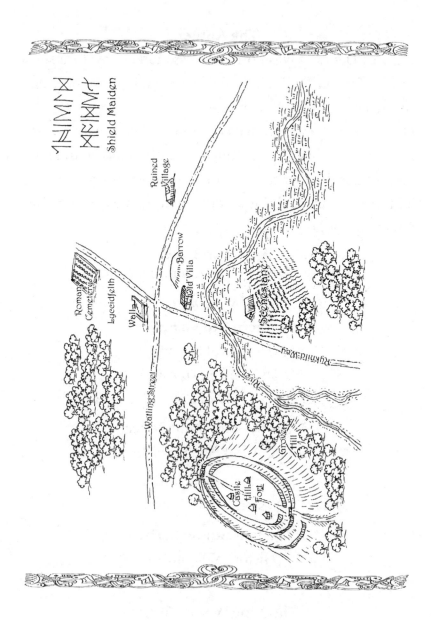

Shield Maiden

CHAPTER ONE
ANNA

"It's not fair!" the girl shouted as she stabbed her short sword down into the oak table, leaving it vibrating in the wood. Her deep green eyes fixed the man on the far side with a furious glare.

"Father, it's not fair! Why can Lar train as a warrior and not me?" she asked him, her arms folded in front of her chest and her foot tapping the reed-strewn floor in impatience.

The man she was talking to sighed, as if this was an almost daily argument, which it was, and as if he despaired of ever getting his way with this, his twelve-year-old daughter, which he did. He stepped forward, pulled the knife out of the table and held it out to the girl, handle first.

"Anna, we have been through all this before. Your brother, Lar will follow me as headman of the village one day and must be a warrior. You in turn will marry a warrior or a lord of another village and raise children."

"Lar is younger than me. I don't see why he should be the leader. Raedann tells me there have been warrior women before now - shield maidens - and even queens and ladies who have led their folk in battle. Why not me?"

Her father, Nerian, looked at her helplessly and, as was

his habit when he was at a loss for words he scratched the bald patch in his brown hair.

"Your father has many cares, child.' These words were spoken by a man standing further down the hall, staring at the embers that burned in the fire pit running the length of the building. 'You should not distress him with these ideas. Nor should you take note of what that tinker, Raedann, says."

This was Iden, the priest of Woden, a fat man with grey hair, who enjoyed mead a little too much and as a result had a large belly and red cheeks. Anna, as well as the other children, thought him stuffy and when he preached found him boring and dull. Nothing like Radeann's fun tales of the gods, of great heroes, of the monsters that lived in the woods and hills and of the adventures he had supposedly had in the world outside their tiny village of Scenestane.

Iden was right in that Raedann was a tinker: he sold trinkets as he travelled around the villages of Mercia. But he sold stories too - anything for a bed for the night and maybe some food and mead. His stories were good ones and the children loved them.

"Are you saying that Raedann lies?"

"Child," Iden replied as he came to join them at the table, "he is a spinner of tales. He exaggerates. He makes stories seem more than they really are."

"But there have been shield maidens," Anna insisted, "women who fight alongside the men."

Iden nodded, but Anna could see he was reluctant to admit it. "Maybe,' he agreed, 'but not many and only when something unusual happens, when special times come along and they are forced to take up arms. It is best to forget such tales. You will soon be old enough to marry. You should be thinking about that and not this nonsense."

"I can be a warrior. I will prove it to you one day!"

"Please, Anna," her father pleaded with her. "Take back your seax and go help Udela prepare the evening meal."

Fists clenched, teeth gritted, Anna glowered at him for a while and then finally let her shoulders drop. Reaching out she removed the long knife which he offered her and slid it into the scabbard on her belt. With a nod she left the headman's hall and walked out into the village. Once there though, she did not go as ordered to the cookhouse to find the elderly cook, but looked around the village, past the wooded path that led up to the rocky outcrop upon which Iden's small temple was built, to the hut that lay beyond. This was home of the healing woman, Julia. Outside it Anna could see her friends loitering, playing a game of Tafel on the ground, with pebbles and a board they had created by cutting lines into the sun-baked mud. She joined them.

Her brother Lar looked up from the game as she approached. He gave her a kindly smile.

"So how did your talk with father go?" he asked, tilting his head towards the headman's hall.

She stuck out her lower lip and frowned at him, "What do you think? You are the boy so you will be leader and a warrior, whilst I have to have babies."

"Sorry, sister, but that is just the way it is," Lar said. "Shield maidens are all well and good in stories, but in the real world we all have to accept what fate has in store for us. If it helps I don't feel any better about it than you, but you can't fight fate."

Anna snorted. "Maybe I can. Maybe I can prove I am worthy to be a warrior and defend the village."

But Lar was not listening to her. He had turned back to the board, smiled and moved one piece.

"My game, pay up Wilburh!"

His opponent, ten-year-old Wilburh, gave Lar a dark look from under a fringe of blond hair, his blue eyes darkened, suddenly seeming almost black.

Wilburh's twin sister, Hild, gurgled with laughter. "Come on, pay him," she said. Her own eyes, whilst also blue, seemed lighter somehow, just like Hild herself - bubbly and happy in a way that gave Anna headaches sometimes and contrasted with Wilburh's more gloomy nature.

Wilburh shrugged and reaching into a pouch at his belt brought out a tarnished old ring and handed it over. Lar held it up to the late afternoon sun and examined it.

"Should be able to sell that to Raedann for a new knife," he boasted.

"A knife? Why in Woden's name do you think that dirty old ring is worth the same as one of my knives," a man's voice cut in.

They turned around and saw the tinker looming over them. Tall, almost gangly, with curly brown hair and a hook nose, Raedann grinned at them. "I will give you this seashell bracelet for it," he said with wink, and Lar and Raedann were soon bargaining and trading.

Listening to her brother Anna shook her head in despair. Lar had no interest in swords and fighting. He had passed on to her all he had learnt after she badgered him into going off to the woods to teach her how to fight with a sword and how to fire a bow. No, Lar was a trader at heart and a good one at that, but he was no fighter. She sighed. If only her father could see that.

"Well, I must be off," Raedann said, after he and Lar had finally agreed a fair exchange for the ring and Lar had got his knife, although not as fine a one as he would have hoped. "I want to reach Wall before the sun sets and that's a couple of miles to go."

The tinker set off towards the Roman road that ran past the west side of the village. Anna beckoned at the children and they all trailed along with Raedann, passing between the blacksmith's house and the one next to it, crossing a field and finally stepping onto the cobbled road beyond.

"We will go to just past the old Roman house with you, Raedann," Anna said. "Tell us about shield maidens again."

Lar groaned. "Not again, sister. Raedann, tell us something different. Tell us about giants."

"Giants? Ah, now there are many sorts of giants in this world. There are hill giants and cliff giants and fire giants and frost ones too. They come from other worlds you know, places like Jotunheim, Niflheim and the fire world, Muspelheim. They visit our world of Midgard from time to time."

He went on telling a tale about how he had once been chased by a fearsome fire giant and had escaped by swimming a river. By the time he had finished they had crossed the ford north of the town where a brook trickled over the old road, and soon they were passing the crumbling ruins of a Roman farm beyond.

"Did the giants build that?" Wilburh asked, gazing at the stone structure.

Raedann smiled at him. "You ask me that because it is made of stone, don't you? But no, the Romans were not giants, just men. They built many houses like that, walls and cities too, all over this land. Then they left because their empire was under attack. That was two hundred years ago. When our own people, the Saxons, came here across the Eastern Sea they gazed on such buildings, and because they could not build them they assumed the Romans must have been giants. That is why those ruins and many others like it make our people feel scared and why we keep away from them."

The children stared at the ruins and Raedann, chuckling at the expressions on their faces, said, "Well, I'll be on my way. I will be back in a couple of days. You'd best be getting home to the village, children. The sun is sinking. You don't want evil spirits to find you out in the dark do you?"

He pointed to where the old fort on the hills to the west was silhouetted against the setting sun. Then he was off, singing a song and strolling up the road.

"Come on, let's go home," Hild said, turning to head back down the road.

Anna moved to join her and then abruptly changed her mind. "No! Let's go and look in the ruins," she said.

"The Roman ruins? In the dark?" Lar asked, studying the decaying structure.

"Indeed, why not?"

The others stared at her. Lar opened his mouth to speak but did not get a word out. Around them the twilight was gathering, the evening air warm but quiet. Into that silence they heard a noise that made them all jump: the sound of running footsteps coming along the road from the direction of the village. They spun around to glance back towards the ford, but could see nothing apart from deep shadows at the bases of the trees.

No, there was something else there.

A shape was moving in the shadows....

CHAPTER TWO
ELLETTE

"**W**hat is it?" Hild asked in a loud whisper.

No one answered her. They were all eyeing the dark shape they could see moving in the shadows at the foot of the trees lining the road. As it came closer, the shape seemed to merge with the nearest tree and then ... it disappeared.

Anna crept closer to the tree, staring intently at where the shape had vanished. She could feel her heart pounding in her chest. The other children held back and peered over her shoulder.

There was dead silence all round, which made what happened next seem even more terrifying.

"HELLO!!" screeched a voice from above their heads.

Once more the children jumped and then they looked up, seeking whoever had spoken. Anna was the first to change from being afraid to annoyed as she spotted what, or rather who, was sitting on a large branch of a tree about ten feet from the ground.

"Ellette! Is that you? What in the name of the gods did you do that for?" Anna shouted up at the small mischievous girl.

Nine-year-old Ellette dropped into view hanging

upside down from the branch, suspended by her bent knees, her head level with Anna's. She stuck out her tongue and then made a rude noise at the older girl.

"Cos I can. You all call me little. But it's not so bad being little you know. I can move around and sneak up on people. So..." she paused and did a small somersault, landing lightly on her sandalled feet, "what are you doing now?"

"We are going to explore the ruins," Lar said. "But you are too young, little elf, so go home."

"The ruins. In the dark? They are haunted aren't they? Great - I'm coming too." Ellette jigged up and down with excitement.

"No, you are not!" Anna said.

Ellette grinned at her. It was not a nice grin. It was a grin that meant, 'Oh yes I am and you might think otherwise, but there is nothing you can do about it!'

"If you don't let me come I am going back to the village and I will tell all your parents where you are!"

"You little tell-tale!" Wilburh said.

"Oh, come on! Let me come along. It's not fair always to be left out," Ellette pleaded, looking up at Anna with puppy-dog eyes.

Anna sighed and glanced around at the faces of the other three. Their expressions suggested that she might as well give in and let the girl join them.

"Oh, very well. But just you do exactly what I tell you to!" she ordered.

Ellette grinned and this time it was a sweet grin that said, 'Of course I will. I am a good girl.'

"If we are going, let's go now," Wilburh said, his gaze lingering on the sun, which was already dipping below the western horizon.

They left the road and headed eastwards towards the ruins, across the flat fields that ran along the north bank of the brook. Beyond the brook, through a small orchard that grew at the top of the village, they could make out the headman's hut, Iden's temple and some of the other village buildings. Smoke rising from several of them appeared inviting. The late summer evening was cooling quickly and looking at the dark shape of the caved-in walls and the collapsed roof of the Roman villa, Anna shivered. She felt suddenly cold, as if something was watching them, something ancient and evil.

"It's just fairy stories and make believe, nothing more," she muttered to herself, but by the time they reached the ditch that ran around the ruined house she was already regretting her rash decision to come here. Why had she suggested it? To prove a point that she was worthy to be a courageous warrior? That seemed ridiculous now. She almost suggested they abandon the expedition altogether, yet she could not turn back now could she? Not without losing face. She could hardly argue with her father about becoming a warrior and then run away, scared by a few old stones.

Anna walked closer to Wilburh. The quiet boy did not say much, but she knew he spoke to Raedann a lot and was always studying runes and scrolls in Iden's temple. She had once asked him if he wanted to be a priest one day. "No," he had replied, "a wizard." She had giggled at the time, but Wilburh seemed so serious and Raedann did tell stories about wizards and magic so maybe it was not so much nonsense after all. As well as trying to learn spells, the boy had learnt a lot from both Raedann and Iden about history, about the tales of the gods and legends about monsters.

"So, do you think the ruins could really be haunted?" she asked him as they crossed the ditch.

"As Raedann says, just because we fear them does not mean there are ghosts," he answered, his tone suggesting she was just a silly girl, but Anna noticed he kept looking nervously at the building.

The way in to the villa was on the east side of the house, so they had to circle the structure, at which point they entered the shadow on the west created by the setting sun. There, in the gloom, they could make out the entrance. In front of them the wooden door of the building was rotten and had fallen inwards revealing a gaping opening into a dark, cave-like interior.

"We need some light," Ellette said.

"Wait a moment," the ever practical Hild replied, stooping to gather some branches and dry leaves that had fallen to the ground at the edge of the nearby woods.

Piling up the leaves and twigs near the doorway into the villa, she reached into her belt pouch and brought out a strike-a-light and a flint. Bending over the kindling she struck the flint against the strike-a-light until sparks flew off it. Some sparks fell upon the leaves and ignited them. She added more twigs and then larger branches, nursing the flame until she had a good fire going. The fire illuminated a hallway just inside the doorway.

Meanwhile, Wilburh had collected some bark and a long stick and wrapping the bark around the stick, secured it with some rushes and weeds. He took from his belt pouch a cube of pig fat wrapped in a dock leaf. "That should do it," he said, daubing the bark with fat. Then, wiping his greasy fingers on his tunic, he thrust the makeshift torch into his sister's fire. Spitting and crackling it ignited and Wilburh held it aloft.

"Who is going first?" he asked.

"Oh me, please!" Ellette offered excitedly.

"Be careful then. I will follow and then Wilburh can come next with the torch," Anna instructed.

"Look out for holes in the ground and make sure the

roof does not fall in on top of you," Lar suggested. "Hild and I will bring up the rear."

Ellette scuttled forward. Lifting one foot she stepped over the threshold and then she was inside, standing in what must have once been the entrance hall. The hall led onwards into a large central courtyard or garden. It was open to the skies and above them the first stars of evening could now be seen, along with the sliver of the moon.

The children all joined her. In the flickering torchlight they could see that around the courtyard were doorways leading into other rooms.

"Where shall we go?" Hild asked, her voice squeaking like a frightened mouse.

"Try those first," Anna suggested, pointing to the doors along the left side.

The first one led to a room containing some rotten sacks and several cracked pots and glass bottles filled with a murky liquid. It seemed to be a store room or pantry. Anna wrinkled her nose at the musty smell. Beyond the sacks they heard a sudden scuttling noise and a large rat ran out across the room and bolted for the door, passing between Lar's feet and disappearing into the night.

"Ugh! I hate rats," Lar grimaced.

The next room seemed to have been the kitchens. The roof had collapsed into it, but they could see the openings of a bread oven at one end and smashed crockery littering the floor.

Along the back of the house was a large room with a beautifully decorated floor. The tiles were made of many different colours, shapes and sizes and together they made a pattern. Wilburh held out the torch so they could examine it. It portrayed animals running through a forest and men chasing them on horseback.

"It's a hunt - see there is a stag and those are boars," Hild said.

Above them there was a sudden commotion and the whir of flapping wings. An instant later Anna felt something fly past her and heard a high-pitched squeaking.

"Bats!" Wilburh shouted. He lifted the torch higher and they could see that where the ceiling over the corner of the room had fallen in, it had revealed the roof cavity above. In the cavity several dozen bats were hanging from the rafters. As the children watched, another pair dropped from the beams and flitted out of the room, passing over Lar's head. He gave a cry of alarm and ducked.

"What is it with all these animals and me?" he complained.

"Let's go home," Hild suggested, sounding even more frightened than she had before.

"But we have not finished yet," Ellette pointed out, her voice still full of excitement. "Let's check the other doors."

Anna nodded and led the way back, out into the

courtyard and across to a door on the north side. She tried to open it but it appeared to be jammed. She gave it a kick but it would not budge.

"Lar, give me some help!" she ordered her brother. He came and stood next to her and together they shoulder-barged the door. It gave a little, but was still stuck.

"One last time!" she shouted and they tried again, charging towards the door. This time it flew open.

Lar and Anna tumbled through the opening into the dark interior and ended up lying sprawled across the damp floor.

"Ouch," Lar said, "I think I've sprained my wrist."

Coming to stand at the doorframe, Wilburh leant forward and held the torch aloft. As the flames lit up the room Anna saw Lar's eyes widen, focusing on something behind her. She started to turn.

"Anna," Lar whispered urgently, "don't move!"

Ignoring his instructions, she turned her head and then froze as she heard a hiss. Not a yard from where she lay, its forked tongue flicking in and out, was the uncoiling body of a large snake, its dark eyes staring right into her own. It hissed again and opened its mouth as if ready to strike.

"Help!" Anna whimpered.

CHAPTER THREE
THE HORN

Suddenly, the sound of whirling filled the room.
"Get down!" Ellette shrieked.

As Anna ducked, a stone flew through the air where her head had been, so close she felt it stir her hair. It smacked into the snake's neck and the creature hesitated, but then drew back to strike. Unable to draw her seax in time, Anna glanced behind and saw Ellette spinning a sling around her head preparing to release another stone. This one missed, whirring past to clatter off the far wall.

The snake lunged.

Recoiling from the snapping fangs, Anna smelt its fetid breath warm upon her cheek.

"Get back, Anna!" Wilburh ordered as he strode forward, one hand still holding the torch and the other held up, palm facing the snake. "*Dēor áflíeh!*" he shouted, advancing towards it.

The creature froze in mid-lunge for a moment, either dazed or confused by the spell. Then it appeared to recover and pulled back in readiness to strike again.

"*Dēor áflíeh!*" Wilburh repeated, and this time the snake recoiled and slithered away towards the dark corner of the room.

The children gaped at the boy in astonishment. 'So it is true,' thought Anna, 'he has been studying magic.' None of them had seen him use it before and it was both frightening and amazing at the same time.

Over in the darkness, the snake hissed once more and Anna, realising this was not the best time to discuss the matter, shouted, "Get out quickly!"

She and her brother scrambled to their feet and started backing away towards the door, but Ellette either had not heard or took no notice. In fact she moved deeper into the room, her gaze flicking to where the snake lay coiled in the corner.

"Ellette, come on!" Anna cried, but the small figure crouched down and scuttled into the opposite corner furthest away from the snake. The creature seemed to be recovering from the charm Wilburh had used upon it, because it started to uncoil and move towards her.

"Ellette, what are you doing? Come on!" Anna repeated, drawing her seax and moving up behind the little girl.

"Just coming," Ellette said. She reached forward and now Anna could see that she had picked something up off the floor: something that glowed in the light cast from Wilburh's torch. Anna stretched out her hand, grasped Ellette by the shoulder and dragged her towards the exit.

The snake put on a spurt and lunged towards them, but Anna swung with her seax and the blade almost caught the creature beneath its head. It rose up, jaws wide, hissing at them in anger, but then retreated once more into the darkness.

"Get out!" Anna shouted and they all scampered back to the doorway. Once in the courtyard they forgot about the two remaining doors and headed towards the main entrance. Anna was last out, guarding the doorway until the others had left the villa and then stepping outside into the circle of light projected by Hild's fire

Once outside she spun round to Ellette. "What on earth were you thinking?" she shouted, but Ellette was not listening. She and the others were focused upon the object she had found in the snake's chamber.

"What is it?" Anna asked, moving forward so she also could get a look. Ellette turned towards her and held up her hands. Cradled within them was an object so beautiful that Anna felt as if she would cry just looking at it. It was in the shape of an ox horn, like those the villagers used to drink mead and ale from, but made of solid gold. Its outer surface bore runes and etchings, shapes and patterns. Anna recognised a wild boar - the symbol of the Goddess Freya - the spear of Woden and the hammer of Thunor, the god of thunder.

"It is wonderful," she said.

"Yes, and worth a pretty sum," Lar added, his eyes full of awe, but also tinged with a touch of greed.

"What... what does it sound like?" Hild asked.

Ellette shrugged and raising it to her lips took a deep breath and blew.

Nothing happened. Not a sound, not a single note.

Puzzled, Anna frowned, but Lar snatched the horn away from Ellette. "You are not blowing it hard enough, little elf," he said. "Let me try." He puffed out his cheeks and blew, but again nothing happened. Not even a peep. Lar blushed and seeing Wilburh was grinning, handed him the horn. "You think you are so smart with all your magic and tricks, you try!"

Wilburh gulped, tried and failed. Hild gave it a go next with the same result, then passed it at last to Anna.

"Looks like it's broken," Anna said, holding the horn in her hand but not trying it. "I mean, it looks nice and all that, but it's just an ornament; it's not meant to make a sound."

"Oh, give it a go, Anna, why don't you," Ellette said.

Anna shrugged and taking a deep breath blew hard, expecting to prove her point. The note that sounded from the horn seemed to start deep in the earth beneath her feet. 'No,' thought Anna, 'deeper even than that.' It was as if it vibrated upwards from the very rocks and stones of Midgard. The sound grew louder and louder as it seemed to shake their bones and rise up through their bodies until it flew out into the air around them and echoed on and on through the skies, even upwards towards the heavens. As the notes died away they all heard something else - a word spoken by a voice just loud enough for them to hear, as if someone had uttered it from afar and it had been carried here on the wind.

The word was '*Chosen*'.

Anna took the horn away from her mouth and stared down at it. The other children gawped at her and the horn too.

"Merciful Woden!" Lar exclaimed. "What was that?"

Before Anna could say anything, the skies above them were shattered by a ferocious burst of light and a terrifying clap of thunder. A moment later the heavens opened and a torrential downpour started.

"Quick," Anna shouted, shoving the horn into her belt, "back to the ford."

The children set off running across the fields towards the Roman road. The rains continued to fall heavily around them and soon the field was like a bog. As they struggled on through the storm, fighting against the driving rain, their feet sinking into ground that with every step was turning into a quagmire, Ellette, who was in the lead, suddenly stopped, screamed and pointed ahead of her.

"What is it?" Anna yelled, trying to make herself heard over the fury of the wind that now howled around them.

"Look!" It was all the small girl could manage as she

gestured again into the gloom.

There was another flash of lightning and there, between the children and the road, was a shape. It was a dog ... a hound as large as a pony. Its fur was jet black; black as only the night can be when there is no moon, or as dark as the deepest caves. The only other colour was in its eyes and these were red like the embers of a fire, glowing as they gazed upon the children. Then the dog growled and they felt terror seep into their bones.

"Another one!" screamed Lar, this time gesturing behind to where another huge hound loomed towards them out of the night.

"Where did they come from?" Hild shrieked, clinging to his arm.

"They are barghests, hell hounds, black dogs," Wilburh replied. "Don't you ever listen to Raedann's tales?" He lifted the torch up above his head, its feeble flames fighting a losing battle against the rain. "*Fulbeorht!*" he shouted and the dying flames burst into a glorious blaze of light illuminating the surrounding fields.

"That's a neat trick!" Lar shouted as the dogs recoiled and fled yelping into the darkness.

"They fear the light, but it will not last long!" Wilburh said. "Come on, we must reach the ford."

Anna nodded and taking the lead from Ellette sprinted hard for the road, but after only twenty paces the torchlight dimmed, flickered and went out. The others all bunched up behind her. Now they were alone in the dark.

Out of sight the dogs howled again. More than two: a dozen maybe, and the children could hear them closing upon them once more. The rain seemed to get heavier and now the children were soaked through, freezing cold and terrified.

"Run!" Anna shouted. For a moment her companions did not move, but stared fearfully into the gloom, waiting for the shapes of the dogs to come at them out of the rain.

"RUN!" bellowed Anna. This time they responded and started running towards the ford. Behind them they could hear the howling changing to growling as the dogs came into sight, once again chasing after them.

The ford was fifty paces away. Anna could see that Ellette was starting to falter, the little figure struggling to keep up the pace. Hild too was panting hard. Forty paces now. Ellette slowed down and began to walk then hobble.

"I've hurt my ankle," she said, when Anna stopped beside her, "please don't leave me!"

Anna looked back at the dogs. Three of them were close now. There was no way the girl would reach the ford before the beasts caught up with her, and even if she did they would just chase her over it.

"Keep running!" she shouted at the others. "Lar, take Ellette!" She pushed the small girl over to her brother.

"What?" Lar said. "What about you?"

Drawing her seax, Anna smiled at him and turned to face the hounds, but Lar, glancing back at them, shook his head. He took Ellette in his arms and passed her on to Wilburh. "Get her across!" he cried, and pulling out his own knife went to stand beside his sister.

Supported by Wilburh, Ellette hobbled down the road, followed by Hild. Behind them Anna and her brother stood side by side, backing slowly towards the ford whilst half a dozen of the snarling hell hounds, their mouths slavering and foaming as they growled and barked, closed in upon them.

CHAPTER FOUR
GUÐRUÐÐ

The dogs came forward snarling at the two children, their outstretched talons clattering and scraping at the cobbles of the road beneath their paws.

Step by step, Anna and Lar backed off towards the ford, their seax held out in front of them threatening to cut down any beast that came within reach. Meanwhile, the torrential downpour continued all around them, soaking the children to their skins and chilling them to the bone, so that they shivered in equal amounts from cold and fear, both thinking that the small blades would not keep the huge Barghests away for long.

They were right.

One of the dogs leapt at Lar. He jumped out of the way, slipped on the slick surface of the wet road and fell flat on his back, jarring his elbow as he hit the ground. His seax went spinning out of his hand and splashed into the swollen waters of the brook. Now defenceless, he faced the dog that had landed beside him and was leaning over him, jaws opening ready to bite.

Anna tried to move across to protect her brother, but a second hound latched onto the hem of her dress and tugged her away from Lar. Lashing out at the animal with her blade she nicked its ear. The hound yelped and released her, but a moment later it was coming on again. Over to her right Lar let out a shout of pain as jaws fastened around his arm.

Suddenly, with an ear-shattering bang, a flash of bright light seemed to burst from just above Anna's head. The light hung there like a miniature sun, growing larger, brighter and more intense. As one, the dogs lifted their heads and howled a loud, doleful cry, full of pain and fear. Then they turned and scampered away, vanishing into the darkness that surrounded the light.

Peering after them, Anna noticed something else: the rain, which until now had been unending, stopped as abruptly as it had begun. The light started to fade and as it did, above them the clouds scattered and the star-strewn night sky came into view.

Anna staggered over to where Lar still lay on the ground and tugged him up by his good arm, observing that his other arm was welling with blood where he had been bitten. Lar was not bothering about his wound, though. Once on his feet he was looking all around in amazement to see that the storm and the dogs had both vanished as if they had never been. "What happened?" he gasped. "Where did they go?"

No one answered: all were just as amazed as he.

"Did you cause that light to appear, Wilburh?" Anna

called. Re-sheathing her seax, she checked that the horn was still tucked safely through her belt then steered Lar across the ford.

Wilburh, who was still supporting Ellette - the pair having reached the other side of the stream - shook his head. "It was nothing to do with me, but it was powerful magic, I can tell you that. The light and that horn: both powerful magic. Maybe we should throw it away..." he suggested, but before they could discuss that idea Lar winced and some blood dripped from his wound onto the road.

"Come here, Lar," Hild said and led the boy to the stream, washing the wound in the cool, clear waters. She then rooted around the edge of the brook and found some sphagnum moss, pressing it to Lar's arm. "Hold it there. I will dress the wound with a salve when we are back in my hut, come on."

The children hurried along the path to the village. As they passed between the houses Anna looked back at the ford. For a moment she saw nothing. Then she spotted movement beside the road on the far side of the brook.

A figure stepped out into the moonlight and turned to look towards the village. At first, Anna thought it was a child or a small woman, but then she saw a beard on the figure's face and realised it was a man: a short man with a long, silvery beard. She could just make out his bushy eyebrows and what looked like a collection of warts on his face to make even ugly old Grandma Sunniva, the oldest woman she knew, seem beautiful.

The man stared towards the village, and with a sudden chill that passed up her spine and lifted the hairs on the back of her neck, Anna realised he was in fact looking directly at her. He took a few more steps out of the wood and pointed at her, so now she knew she was right: he was looking at her! Then he beckoned, gesturing to Anna that she should join him.

"Anna! Where have you been? What happened to you and the other children? You are drenched!"

Brought up short by the sound of her father's voice, Anna swung round. He was standing beside the healing women's hut where she could see Lar having his wound dressed. Ellette, meanwhile, was being helped by Wilburh into the blacksmith's, and by the sound of the scolding she was getting from her mother, Tate, the little girl was also being asked awkward questions.

"Er ... we were caught in the rain, Father," Anna replied, deciding to keep it simple.

"Rain? What rain?"

Anna stared at him as if he were a madman. Only then did she realise that the ground inside the village was bone dry. How was that possible when just a few paces away they had been caught in a ferocious rainstorm? She felt the horn at her hip. Powerful magic, Wilburh had said. What was it? Was it magical? Did it really have power? If so what could it do? And why had it only sounded for her? She wanted to find out, but she did not wish her father or the other villagers to know about it until she had answers. Covering the horn with her hand so no one would see it, she inched it out of her belt and slid it into the sleeve of her dress, out of sight of prying eyes.

Her father was still waiting for an answer, his puzzled frown changing into an angry scowl. "Well, Lar won't say anything either. So if you have both lost your tongues, maybe cleaning all the pots and pans after dinner tonight will help you find them," he snapped. "Go get the meal ready and we will talk again tomorrow!"

Anna nodded and together with her brother she hastened across the village towards the headman's hall. As she did so, she risked another glance back at the ford. The starlit road beyond the brook was in plain sight, but empty. Of hounds, rain and strange little men there was no sign.

Lar saw where she was looking and following her gaze frowned at her. "What are you looking at?" But Anna just shrugged in return and the two of them headed off to do their chores, Anna pushing the horn even further up her sleeve.

The following morning it did rain in the village and the children, along with the villagers, stayed indoors. They all busied themselves with indoor jobs, mending torn tunics, sorting through the stores of smoked meats and cheeses or sharpening knives and tools. Nerian again asked his children about the previous day, how they had got wet and how Lar had got bitten. Anna lied and said they had fallen in the brook when playing a game and Lar made up a story about being chased by a wild dog in the woods, which was almost true. Neither of them wanted to say they had been in the ruins and certainly they did not want to let on about the horn.

The midday meal in the village was the main one of the day and all the villagers came together into Nerian's hall and drank ale or mead and ate the dish prepared by Udela, the cook. Today it was a trio of geese, which had been put into floured bags with herbs, milk and butter and boiled in a cauldron. Anna was expected to help and assisted in plucking the birds and cutting up the vegetables. Alongside the geese they had cooked beans, barley, turnips and leeks, each in their own little bag hanging down into the same cauldron. The goose meat was carved and served out with helpings of the boiled vegetables along with a sweet sauce made from plums and apples.

They all tucked into the meal, dabbing up the juices with bread, which had been cooked fresh that morning to accompany it. The food made Nerian mellow and as a result he permitted the children some time to themselves whilst he slept off the meal.

Once the rain had stopped, Anna led them out of the hut and into the orchard, where they each picked apples and munched them sitting on a fallen tree trunk.

"What have you done with the horn, Anna?" Lar asked. It was the first time they had been alone since returning to the village.

In answer she pulled it from out of the pouch she wore at her belt. The noon sun caught the gold, which glittered and glowed, lighting up Anna's face as though she were sat in candlelight or in front of a fire.

They all stared at it for a while and then Lar asked a question. "Shall we sell it? It would be worth a fortune, a treasure like that."

Wilburh sighed. "It is magical, surely you can see that after what happened ... after last night?"

Lar looked unconvinced. "What happened last night? It rained on us and some dogs attacked us and lucky for us the lightning frightened them away. That is all. Doesn't mean the horn is magical all of a sudden. But it is made of gold and that means it is worth a lot."

"Lar, really," Wilburh frowned. "Why could only Anna blow it and the rest of us not? Surely you can see something odd was happening?"

"What's odd?" Lar shrugged. "It's an old horn we found

in a ruined building. It was probably blocked with rubbish. We all had a blow and by the time Anna tried, it had got unplugged and made a sound, that's all."

"Are you really that stupid, Lar!" Wilburh sneered.

Leaping to his feet Lar approached the other boy. "Come here and say that again," he said, fists bunched.

"Stop it!" Hild jumped up and got between the two boys. "Don't fight please!"

They were distracted by Ellette, who had stood up and was hobbling past them, one ankle still strapped up. "Look! Who's that?" she said, pointing into the village.

They all looked. Scenestane seemed just as quiet as it usually did during the midday meal and for an hour or so afterwards, whilst the villagers were all still finishing their food and planning the afternoon's work. Despite this, the children could see that one figure was at large and walking around the hovels. It was no one they recognised and after watching for a moment, Anna was sure it was the same little man she had seen on the road the previous evening. The warty fellow was sneaking around the buildings, peering into the interiors and then, apparently disappointed, moving on to the next.

"Who is it?" Hild asked the question they were all thinking.

"Ugly fellow isn't he?" said a voice at their backs, making them all jump. It was Raedann the tinker, who had crept up right behind them.

"Merciful Woden, Raedann, you scared us half to death!" Ellette said.

"Sorry about that, but I saw you from the road and thought I would see what you were up to."

"We are watching that fellow at the moment," Anna pointed. "Do you know who he is?" As Raedann looked where she pointed, she slipped the horn back into her pouch hoping he had not noticed it, but she could not be certain.

"Him, oh he is Gurdrunn. I see him from time to time.

He lives over in the hills to the west," Raedann said, then frowned and squinted towards the little man. "Odd thing is, you don't see him out much. He and his kind are not much interested in the affairs of men, you see."

Anna turned to stare at Raedann. "What do you mean 'his kind'? Is he Welsh or Irish or something like that?"

Raedann laughed. "Indeed not. He comes from much further away than that. Beyond the bounds of Midgard."

"Outside Midgard! You mean he is not human, not from Earth?"

"No, he is from Nidarvellir."

Wilburh gasped, but the other children looked confused.

"Where is that?" Ellette asked, her eyes now wide with the excitement she always felt when listening to Raedann's tales.

"Nidarvellir? Have I never told you? Well, it's the world of the dweorgs, little one: Gurdrunn is a dwarf."

CHAPTER FIVE
KENDRA

The dweorg continued to sneak about the village and it seemed to the children that he was almost sniffing at each door, like a dog after a bone.

"What's he doing?" Anna asked.

Raedann shrugged. "I don't know. Dweorgs are strange fellows, but talented too. They spend their time down mines digging up precious metals and stones and making them into beautiful objects. Wondrous and magical items too. Things like Thunor's hammer and Woden's rings, and also Freya's necklace, the Brisingamen."

The tinker laughed. "It is almost as if he has lost one of his treasures the way he is carrying on. I think I will go and see what he wants. Dweorgs can get mighty angry if they lose something magical. I wouldn't want any harm coming to old Nerian or any of your folk."

"Anna ..." Hild gasped, her eyes wide and frightened, but Anna gave a quick shake of her head to silence her. She knew what the younger girl was trying to say. Did the horn belong to Gurthrunn and if so, would he be angry at them for taking it? Anna began to wonder if he already suspected that she had it. After all, he had been staring at her so very intently last night.

"Oh, Raedann, please don't go," Anna caught hold of the tinker's arm. "Tell us about ... tell us about Barghests. Have you ever met one?"

Raedann's eyes widened and he shivered, despite the warmth of the afternoon sun. Then he smiled and removing Anna's hand from his sleeve, sat back against a tree. "Have a mind for tales of scary monsters do you? Well indeed, the black dogs are frightening enough. There is something otherworldly about them and they are like some spirit come from Helheim. Yet they are solid enough and their fangs and claws can inflict real harm."

Exchanging glances with Lar, Anna noticed he was holding his wounded forearm while he listened, the bandages hidden under his tunic.

"Why do they appear? What are they after?" she asked, trying to make the question sound innocent enough, but Raedann gave her an odd look as if he was wondering why she was asking.

"Well, in some cases folk say they carry messages of doom and they appear to people who are going to die soon."

"Die?" Hild muttered fearfully.

Raedann nodded, "Other times they seem drawn to crossing places - crossroads, fords, mountain passes, borders and so on. Indeed, they seem attracted to these locations as if they sense movement from one place to another."

"Are they magical?" Ellette asked.

"Certainly, or at least they are drawn by magic, particularly magic to do with comings and goings, travel and so forth."

Raedann gave Anna another long stare. "Why all these questions - dweorgs, black dogs, magic - eh? It seems to me that you have something on your mind. Do you want to let me know what it is?"

"Er...," Anna mumbled, unsure what to say. She stared at the others. Hild just looked frightened, which was not unusual. Ellette was excited and Anna was concerned that the little girl might just come out and tell Raedann the whole story. The two boys both shook their heads, for once in agreement about something, although Anna suspected they had different reasons for not wanting to tell Raedann about the horn. Lar was probably still trying to decide how much he could sell it for and Wilburh was keen to know more about its powers.

The tinker stared at each of them in turn in a way that seemed to suggest he knew something was going on, and then he smiled. "Very well, I won't pry."

He jumped up from the ground and started back towards the road, calling over his shoulder, "I am off south. I will be back in a couple of days. If you want to talk then, I will be happy to listen." He gave a wave and was off walking through the trees, singing to himself.

Anna looked after him and then back at the village, but of the dwarf, Gurthrunn, there was no longer any sign. There was, however, someone else. A rider, who as she watched, dismounted from a white stallion and stood beside it glancing around as if waiting for someone to notice her presence.

"Who's she?" Ellette squeaked, gazing at the woman who now stood in the centre of the village.

The contrast with the little man who had been there moments before could not have been more striking. She was an imposing figure, tall and startlingly beautiful, and at the same time giving the impression of possessing great strength. Her long, blonde, almost silvery hair cascaded onto her shoulders and down her back. Her gown was pale blue, with a silvery pattern at her wrists and down her front. Over this she had thrown a cloak of deeper blue, which was fastened at one shoulder by a silver brooch. Around her neck there hung an amulet that caught the sun's light and glittered with all the colours of the rainbow.

"Whoever she is, she is beautiful," Lar said.

Someone had clearly spotted the lady, for now they saw Nerian coming out of the headman's hall to stand in front of her. He gave her a respectful bow and it was plain to see that he and the other villagers, who now emerged to join him, believed her to be a woman of rank: perhaps an earl's wife or even a queen. At that moment Nerian, his head jerking left and right as if searching for someone, looked straight at Anna and waved at her and the other children to join him.

They did so, running back through the orchard and pushing through the throng of villagers that now surrounded Anna's father and the stranger.

"Ah, Anna, there you are. Now this," Nerian gestured to the woman, "is the Lady Kendra. She is a noblewoman who is travelling north and she has asked us for hospitality and a bed for the night. Take care of her horse and see that it is fed. Lar, open up Gwen's old hut and light a fire to drive the damp away."

Anna exchanged glances with her brother. Gwen, when almost as old as Grandma Sunniva, had died in her hut earlier that summer and no one had yet taken it over.

"Yes, Father," Lar nodded and went with Ellette to collect firewood.

Nerian turned his attention back to the woman. "If you would come with me, my Lady, "I will offer you some food and drink at my table while the hut is being made ready for you."

Lady Kendra inclined her head and without so much as a glance at the children, glided after Anna's father and disappeared into the hall.

Meanwhile, Hild and Wilburh went with Anna, who led the horse around the back of the blacksmith's to the small paddock, which enclosed the only two horses the villagers owned. Both were mares, small and shaggy compared to Lady Kendra's magnificent animal.

Admiring the stallion's clean lines and alert gaze, Anna removed the saddle and bridle, murmured a few words into the stallion's flickering left ear then let him loose, smiling as he squealed at the two mares. They whinnied a noisy reply and came trotting over, their hooves throwing up clods of mud in their haste to inspect the stranger.

"That Kendra seems a bit cold if you ask me," Hild observed. "Didn't say a word to any of us, she didn't even look at us."

Anna shrugged, still smiling at the three horses as they set off at a gallop around the paddock, tails held high. "I imagine she is just tired after her journey from wherever it is she has come."

"That is the odd thing, though, Anna. It is still only early afternoon. Why stop here for the night when she could easily reach Lyccidfelth before dark?" Hild said.

"Another thing, too," Wilburh commented, "don't you think it is odd for a lady like her to travel alone? She would not be safe out on the road without an escort. That amulet alone must be worth a fortune."

Anna did not reply because she had just noticed that Nerian, Meccus and all the men in the village had emerged from the headman's hall and were hurrying over to the blacksmith's home. They reappeared a few moments later carrying shovels, pickaxes and a variety of other tools. Without any word from Nerian, they all marched out of the village towards the road, passing Lar and Ellette, who had just come out of Gwen's hut and were staring after them.

"What's going on?" murmured Wilburh.

"No idea," Anna replied. Puzzled, they ran over to join Lar and Ellette and buzzing with curiosity, the five children followed at a distance.

The group of men walked purposefully to the ford then split into two. Most carried on up the road in the direction of Wall. Others, led by Meccus, peeled off towards the ruined villa that Anna and the others had explored the day before.

"What are they up to?" Lar asked, frowning in confusion.

"I've no idea," Anna repeated, thinking that Lars was right to be confused. As Raedann had pointed out, everyone believed the Roman ruins were haunted so avoided them. She and the other children had always been told to stay away and yet today, Meccus and the others marched right up to the crumbling building and without stopping, pushed the rotted door out of their way, stepped over it and soon started clattering and banging around inside.

Scuttling up to the villa, Anna peered through the doorway, mystified to see the men were moving blocks of stone that had collapsed from the walls, and sifting through the debris from a caved-in roof.

Meccus turned and before Anna could dodge back he saw her at the door.

She cleared her throat, "Ah, Meccus, do you know where my father is?" she asked innocently, wondering if the men knew about the snake and whether she should warn them.

He looked at her blankly and seemed to be struggling to answer. "He has gone to Wall, to dig," he said after a moment.

"Are you all right, Meccus? You seem a bit, er ... distant."

"I am ... fine. Go away. I need to get back to digging."

"Digging for what, Father?" asked Ellette, who had pushed up behind Anna.

"We need to find it you see," Meccus said distractedly, not answering his daughter's question.

"Find what?" she asked again.

At first, Meccus's gaze seemed to go straight through her, but after a moment he blinked and gave her a look of recognition. "Ah, Ellette, hello. Be careful, it is dangerous here."

"Father! What are you looking for?" she shouted, exasperated.

"Looking for?" Meccus, his expression suggesting she was slow-minded, added, "Why, child - the horn, of course. The horn. And when we find it, we will give it to Kendra."

chapter six
the horn

"What's going on, Anna?" Ellette asked. "What's wrong with my father? He seems so strange, like he's in some kind of daze. "

The children had retreated from the villa, finding a quiet glade in the woods to sit and talk.

"I don't know," Anna replied.

Ellette plucked a stem of grass and stuck it between her teeth. "Who is this Kendra woman do you suppose, and how did she know about the horn?"

"Yes," Lar frowned, "and what did she say to Father to persuade him just moments after she arrived to take the men out to dig in the villa, and even worse, up at Wall," he shivered.

"I've never been to Wall," Ellette said. "What's wrong with it?"

"You must have heard the stories."

Ellette, always ready to hear them again, grinned at him. "Remind me."

Lar pushed his back against a tree and lowered his voice trying to sound like Raedann. "It's haunted by the restless spirits of a people long dead. It was a settlement built by the Romans at the junction of two of their great roads centuries ago, long before we Saxons came here. The legions had a fort there, but it's in ruins now, just like the mouldy old villa outside Scenestane. It was our ancestors who called the town 'Wall', the Romans had another name for it ... but I can't remember it ..." he stumbled to a halt.

"Letocetum was the name," Wilburh said, looking pleased with himself, but the only response this got from Lar was a scowl at the interruption.

"Anyway, according to the stories it was already crumbling when our folk first came from across the sea and built the village eighty years ago. Our great-grandfathers built their houses of wood and thatch, but Wall, like the villa, was made of cold stone. It's heavy and hard and lots of the Romans' slaves died working with it – or so Raedann says. It is probably they who haunt it now, buried beneath it where they fell."

"I heard another story," Wilburh interrupted again, "that there was a battle near Wall a hundred years ago between the first Saxons and the Welsh and all the bodies were buried there or nearby in that old Roman cemetery. It is their ghosts who come out at night, not the slaves."

Lar did not seem impressed. "Maybe. But whatever the story, our people have always kept far away from the place ... well, until today that is. That's why no Saxons live there and they are building that new town up at Lyccidfelth.

"So why are they going there now?" Ellette asked in a

small voice.

No one could answer.

"What about the horn? How did Kendra know it was here?" Hild wondered out loud.

"Yes and why does she want it? What does it do that makes her so keen to find it?" Wilburh commented.

"Maybe it does nothing, but she has heard of it and knows it is worth a lot," Lar suggested with a sideways glance at the younger boy.

Wilburh sighed, "Do you really think she is after it just because it is made of gold? Surely you know it has magical powers? We all heard it speak - say that word, 'chosen' - whatever that meant."

"And don't forget that odd little dwarf, Gurthrunn," said Anna. "Raedann says they sense magical items and there he was, sniffing around the hut the day after he saw me with the horn at the ford."

"Raedann might tell us more if we showed him the horn," Hild said.

"He might, but he is away at the moment," Anna pointed out.

"Well ... we could try and speak to Iden. He might know something about all this," Wilburh suggested. "He does not use magic himself, but I learnt some of what I can do from his scrolls and he knows more about the old stories than anyone else. Maybe he would know what the horn is.

I did not see him leaving the village with the others. I think he must still be in the temple."

Anna nodded. She could not recall seeing the priest of Woden leave his temple and join her father and the other men, so maybe Wilburh was right. She jumped up and stood looking down at them, "Very well, let's go. But let's be careful. With everyone acting so odd I don't know who to trust."

"You can trust Iden. He's a bit stuffy, but he is a good man. He won't harm us," Wilburh said.

The children walked down out of the woods and through the orchard into the village. All was quiet. The men were away digging in the Roman ruins; the women were at first nowhere to be seen, but as they passed the headman's hall Anna glanced inside and her jaw dropped at what she saw.

All the women in the village, along with the youngest children, were sitting in a circle around the headman's high-backed chair – her father's chair. Anna stifled a shout of outrage when she saw Kendra sitting in it as if she were the ruler of the village and not Nerian. What was even more odd was that the village women did not seem to mind. At any other time they would have taken great offence to a stranger assuming such authority and taking such liberties. But not on this day. They were quiet and attentive and just sat gazing up at Kendra with what looked like adoration -

as if she were ... well, as if she were a goddess!

"Look!" Anna hissed. The others all looked inside and gasped.

Perhaps feeling the children's shocked gaze upon her, Kendra glanced up and saw Anna. Her expression was neither welcoming nor angry, it was simply disinterested, as if Anna and her companions were of no importance. After a moment, the beautiful woman looked away and continued to stare down at her ring of admirers.

Mystified, the children hurried away, seeing no one else as they crossed the green to the wooded hill that stood at the east side of the village. A gloomy path led between the overhanging ancient oaks, elms and beeches and climbed up the gentle slope to emerge on the hill top. Here, in a sacred grove, stood the little temple where the villagers worshipped the gods. When they reached the entrance they hesitated outside. Ellette put an ear to the door.

"Is he in there?" Anna asked.

"I can't hear anything, let me check," her friend answered and scuttled around the corner of the temple. Here there was a hidden opening in the wall. A small crack had appeared there - a weakness in the wattle and daub. The children had discovered it when they had been sitting at the rear of the temple during one of Iden's long and boring sermons. Picking at it, Ellette had found that she could push the gap wider from the inside or the outside, making it just big enough to squeeze through. Once, whilst all the grownups' eyes were closed in prayer, the five of them had used it to escape the sermon and go fishing! None of the villagers had yet discovered it and the children treated it as their own secret escape route – or had until recently, but now, apart from Ellette they were all too big.

The little girl pushed at the wall and a small section creaked slightly as it opened. She peeped through the gap then ran back to the others. "He is in there all right," she said in a loud whisper.

They peered through the doorway into the gloomy interior of the temple. As their eyes got used to the darkness inside, they could make out the figure of Iden sitting at the far end. He was bent over a table piled with scrolls, one of which he was reading by the light of the single beeswax candle that stood on the altar beside him. These holy scrolls were covered in runes that recorded the tales of the gods. Only Iden could read them fully, for apart from Wilburh, no one else in the village understood the runic symbols.

"Iden?" Wilburh called, entering the room first. The old man did not look up. As they approached they could hear him muttering, but could not make out the words.

"Iden?" Anna said, but again the priest did not answer.

"Lies ... they are all lies," he muttered, loud enough now to be heard.

"What are lies?" Wilburh asked, but still the old man

would not look at them.

"The gods are false, the holy writings are corrupt, they mention nothing of Kendra," he continued. "They lie. Lie!" Now his voice was growing excited and angry at the same time. "All lies!" he shouted again and gathering up the scrolls thrust them towards the candle flame.

"Iden!" Wilburh cried and seized the priest by the sleeve of his tunic, pulling his arm away from the flames. Iden glared at his novice.

"Let me go Wilburh. I must burn the false writings."

The two were struggling now. The boy was pulling the man's arm away from the flame, desperate to save the scrolls. The priest, older but more frail, fought back. Suddenly Wilburh's grip slipped. He let go of Iden's sleeve and with a cry tumbled back. At the same time the scrolls flew out of Iden's hands, rose high in the air and then flapped and floated back down to earth.

The old man watched them fall and made no effort to stop them. Anna bent forward to scoop them up and as she did so, the horn tumbled out of her pouch and rolled onto the ground near Iden's feet.

The priest looked down, saw the horn and lunged for it, but Anna was faster. Now, ignoring the scrolls, she retrieved the treasure and backed off with it cradled in her arms.

"Girl ... give me that!" Iden commanded with a gesture

at the horn.

"Why? I found it. It's mine," she refused, with a shake of her head.

"Do not be a silly girl. Do as I say!" Iden demanded as he came towards her holding out his arms.

"I am not a silly girl, Iden," Anna said, her voice dangerous now.

"It is not yours, it is Kendra's. It belongs to her and I must give it back to her!"

The priest intoned the words as if he were reciting a prayer or repeating by rote something he had been told. He took a step forward and his foot landed on one of the scrolls, crushing it under his sole.

Wilburh's face went pale. "Iden, you taught me to respect the writings. You are damaging one of the scrolls." He reached down to pull the papers out from under the priest's foot.

Iden gave a dismissive glance downwards. "They don't matter. They are false. Woden, Thunor, Freya, Tiw - all of them are impostors. Only Kendra is a goddess. Only her - and he that she serves."

Wilburh shook his head. "Iden, think what you are saying. You are our priest. You serve the Aesir. The gods speak through you."

Iden snarled. "The gods only lie! Now give it to me!" He lunged towards Anna, his face a mask of rage. She backed off towards the door, staring in amazement at the priest. She could never recall the old man losing his temper. He was set in his ways, stuffy and a bit boring, but not violent. Yet somehow the kindness was gone and all that was left was anger. Whatever strangeness was going on in Scenestane, it was affecting Iden as well.

The other children were just as confused. Wilburh was still on his knees, having retrieved the sacred scrolls, and was now staring up at his master in bewilderment. Lar was standing beside Anna, his hands held out to Iden, trying to keep him away, but not sure that he should lay a hand on a priest. Hild and Ellette had backed off right out of the temple and peered fearfully around the door frame. All of them seemed frozen by the old man's transformation.

"We have to go!" Anna shouted to the others. "Wilburh, leave the scrolls!"

Her words seemed to break the spell and with one look at her, they took to their heels and made for the door, Wilburh, with a regretful sigh, pushing the scrolls carefully under a bench where they would not be trampled.

"Come back here!" Iden yelled after them. "Give me Kendra's horn. Give it to me!" he bellowed as he burst out through the door into the sacred grove.

"Run!" Anna shouted, thrusting the horn back into her pouch, but the children did not need to be told. With little Ellette scampering along in front and Wilburh bringing up the rear they scuttled down the path back to the village green.

"The horn! Bring it back!" They could hear Iden shouting as he started to follow them.

Anna looked towards the headman's hall but could see none of the occupants from this distance. "Whatever is going on here, that Kendra woman is at the centre of it. We must get away from the village and her," she panted, "but where can we go?"

"This way! We can hide in the wheat," Ellette shouted, running to the south side of the village where lay the land the villagers farmed, growing their corn and vegetables in long strips across the ground, which they tilled with the aid of two old oxen.

Following Ellette, the children plunged into the wheat and kept their heads down. The crop had been sown in the early spring and was now tall, the ears swollen and ripening ready for the harvest that would be only a few weeks away.

Here they hid, but it was only a brief respite, for in a short while they heard people spilling out of the village and coming towards them.

"They went this way," Iden's voice sounded. "After them!" he commanded.

The children gasped as they realised that Iden had got all the women from the village out looking for them and by the sound of it, the womenfolk were thrashing at the wheat, deliberately beating it down as they moved closer and closer ....

CHAPTER SEVEN
FLIGHT

"Come on, this way. Quickly!" Ellette hissed and led them towards the ditch that marked the southern edge of the land belonging to the village.

Bending over to stay lower than the top of the wheat, the children scampered through it until they reached the ditch. They slid down into it, splashed across the trickle of a brook that ran along the bottom and then reached the barrier formed by a wild tangle of blackberry bushes on the far side.

Behind them they could still hear the commotion as the search for them continued. Anna felt really odd. They were being chased by their mothers, grandmothers and aunts - people who loved and cared for them - led by Iden who was supposed to watch over them all, and yet, hearing them beating down the corn and having seen the rage and madness in the priest's eyes, she was suddenly terrified of being captured.

Ellette had found the gap in the bushes that the children used when playing in the woodlands to the south of Scenestane and was already through it, followed by Wilburh, Hild and finally, Anna and Lar. On the far side lay a sheltered dell, a dip of ground overshadowed by huge oak trees. Here they crouched down and caught their breath.

"We should be safe here," Ellette said.

"Unless one of the grownups remembers playing here when they were children," Wilburh commented gloomily.

"You are a cheerful boy aren't you?" Lar said.

"He has a point, though," Anna put in. "Even if they don't, what if they ask one of the little ones. Do any of them know of this place?" She looked around the shadowy glade at the other four.

"I ... I think my cousin Martha might remember. I brought her berry picking here last autumn," Hild said.

She had no sooner spoken than they heard a shout from beyond the bushes and an answering call from further away.

"Let's go!" Anna said, and this time she led the way, running further into the woods, hurtling through brambles that snagged their clothing and tugged at their hair. Hild yelped as thorns whipped across her face leaving a gash that started to bleed.

They pressed on through more trees until they burst out onto the road a fair way south of the ford. Panting, they stopped to gaze northwards, but as yet could see no sign of any pursuit.

"Well hello!" a voice called behind them.

All five of them jumped in shock and turning around

saw Raedann standing not ten yards away, leaning on a staff and studying them. The children stared back, afraid to speak, not sure if Raedann was affected by the same spell that Kendra seemed to have woven over all the adults in the village.

"Raedann?" Anna said tentatively.

"Yes, it's me," he answered with a smile.

"Are you ... all right?"

"Of course I am all right!" he answered. "Why wouldn't I be?"

Anna turned her head and whispered to the others, "What do you think?"

Wilburh shrugged, "He seems himself."

"How can we be certain?" Lar put in.

"We have to trust someone, we can't run forever," Hild gasped, still breathless.

"Can I help?" Raedann asked. Whilst they had been talking he had walked up to them and was standing right behind Anna. She turned back to stare into his face then took a deep breath and spoke.

"Raedann, we need to show you something." She looked around at the woods further west across the road. "But not here. Over there, come on," she pointed and making for the trees, reached down and pulled the horn from her belt as she ran.

"So, what do you think?" Anna asked a few minutes later. They were standing in another hidden glade deep in the woods. Raedann was examining the horn. Even in the subdued light the instrument glowed with a golden light that seemed to radiate from it as he turned it over and over in his hands, examining the strange runes inscribed upon it. He shook his head.

"These are not Anglish runes - not our language. Yet they are similar," he said at last as he squinted at them. "I think ... I think they are Dweorgar. Not human. Not then from Midgard, but perhaps forged in Nidarvellir - the world of the dwarves. These words here are all that I can recognise and they say something like 'Use to summon greatness'. Or ...." He hesitated and then said, "Yes, something like 'Blow to summon mighty aid.'"

"What do you mean it is not from our world?" Anna stared at the horn. "How did it get here?"

"There are many who travel between the Nine Worlds, who climb up and down Yggdrasil: the world tree. It came here with one of them maybe. Or was stolen or captured in battle. I do not know. Perhaps Gurthrunn would know. I think you should go to him."

Anna shook her head, "I am not sure. We don't know him. How do you know you can trust him?"

"Oh, I did not say I trusted him," Raedann laughed. "Not completely. He has his own reasons for being here and his own ideas of right and wrong. But he is not evil. Point is, child, who else can you trust when the world you thought you knew has turned upside down and those you love hunt you down? This Kendra woman you talk about? She seems to have your people under her spell. Would you trust her?"

Anna looked at the other children, "What do you think?"

"Everything changed when we found that horn, Anna," Lar said. "The dogs attacked, Kendra appeared and the villagers all altered. You only have to think how the men looked when they went off to dig, like they were under a spell. It has to be something to do with the horn. Maybe ... I don't know ... maybe Gurthrunn would know why."

"I suppose we don't have any choice," Anna nodded. "If this is made by the dwarves then maybe only Gurthrunn can help us. Come on, let's go see him. Raedann, can you lead the way?"

"Of course. He lives in the old fort atop the hills to the west of here. Come, I will show you."

They headed off deeper into the forest, avoiding the farmsteads that lay to the west of Scenestane. From stories Raedann had told in the past Anna knew he meant the hilltop fortress of the old folk, those who had lived in these parts hundreds of years before her own people came here.

As they walked along, Raedann spoke of the land as it had been before the Romans invaded, full of mysterious Celts, druids and warlords, who made weapons of bronze and who had built barrows - underground tombs covered by mounds of turf - in which to bury their dead.

"It is these folk who made the fort we travel to. Our ancestors found it long abandoned, ransacked and conquered by the Romans maybe, and already being reclaimed by the woodlands and wilds. Such places are welcome refuges for those not of our race: elves and dwarves and others. We must be careful ... we must be wary," he said, stopping to peer up into the sky, staring for a moment and then carrying on along the path.

They seemed to have been walking for ages. Above them, the sun had started on its journey to the western horizon, casting long shadows as they hurried along. Wilburh caught up with Anna. "What do you think the villagers will do when Iden tells them we have the horn?"

"I wish you had not said that," Anna said, although she had in fact been thinking the same thing. Normally, if her father found out she had gone beyond the village border, she would get a thrashing or be given extra chores. But nothing was as it had been before the mysterious Kendra had arrived and goodness knows how her father would react now. It didn't bear thinking about.

"What is it, Raedann?" Hild asked, for Raedann was

again pausing to look up into the skies. Whenever the trees parted above them he seemed to be searching for something.

"I am not sure ... I thought I saw something. Come on, let's carry on," was his only answer.

They continued along the path. The ground had started to climb, rising slowly towards the hills a few hundred feet above Scenestane.

Sometime later, when the westering sun had begun to turn the clouds pink, they reached the edge of the trees. Here the forested area was interrupted by a number of large strips of barley and wheat surrounded by grassland. Scattered farmhouses were visible a couple of hundred yards in both directions, but to keep in the cover of the woods would mean going a long way out of their way, so Raedann took a short cut, leading them out across the grass.

On the far side, the ground climbed more steeply and on the nearest hill they could see, half hidden amongst a belt of trees, the old earth fort they were making for. Built in three levels, one above the other, each level had once been protected by a wooden palisade, but as they got nearer, even in the fading light Anna could see that these were now mostly decayed and rotten.

"That is where we are heading," Raedann said, turning to face them all and smiling encouragement at Ellette. "Won't take us long now, little one ..." His voice trailed off and he gawped up at the sky.

Anna swung round to look in the same direction. At first all she could see was a single dot far away. Then it was joined by other dots, five more ... no, ten. No - more than ten - there were twenty now! The dots came closer and grew larger until they were black shapes in the sky. Then, as they closed upon the children, the shapes became clearer and Anna saw they had wings and beaks. They were birds: huge black ravens in full flight and swooping towards them. Anna's heart lurched in her chest, because everyone knew ravens were omens. A single raven might suggest someone was about to die or that a king might lose a battle. But twenty all together? It could only mean something truly terrible was about to happen.

"Run!" Raedann yelled.

And run they did!"

CHAPTER EIGHT
SVARTÁLFAR

The dark shapes sped through the evening skies towards Raedann and the children, who were now running as fast as they could towards the tree line at the bottom of the hills ahead of them.

Ellette was the smallest, but also the most nimble on her feet and was first into the trees, turning back to wave the others on. Hild, bringing up the rear, was wheezing and panting for breath. Anna stopped and leaned across to help the younger girl along, but as she bent forward the golden horn stuck out from her belt so that it was in plain view.

With a triumphant cry, one of the ravens tilted in mid-flight, banked and swooped downwards, claws and talons extended, reaching for the horn.

"Look out, Anna!" Lar shouted a warning and swung wildly with his seax at the diving bird. The creature squawked in protest, snapped angrily at Lar and then, with a couple of mighty beats of its wings, was up and away again. It rejoined its companions, which now circled the children, passing over their heads to perch in the swaying tree tops.

Anna, Hild and Lar caught up with the others and

stood for a moment panting hard. They stared up at the ravens that were now high up in the trees all around them, jumping from one branch to another and making a terrible racket crowing and calling out.

"What are they doing?" Lar shouted over the din.

"They are sending a message," replied Raedann, "telling their master ... or mistress, that we are here. Come, we must reach Gurthrunn."

He led the way deeper into the woods and up the slope that rose towards the hill fort. The birds followed, still crying out in their strident voices as they flitted and jumped from tree to tree.

As she ran along behind Raedann, Anna was sure she caught something moving out of the corner of her eye, but when she turned her head there was nothing other than trees and brambles to see. Another fifty paces or so and it happened again. This time as she spun round to look, Anna spotted something dart behind a tree. Was it a person hiding there? She was about to call out to Raedann when Ellette squealed and pointed behind them.

"There is someone chasing us, but they keep hiding when I looked straight at them," she said.

"I saw them too, but over that way," Anna confirmed with a gesture towards the south. Raedann peered in the same direction, but now there was no movement to spot. He opened his mouth to say something when Hild seized his wrist and pointed to the north.

"Over there, some sort of people, small and with dark-coloured skin."

Raedann nodded and frowned, "Ah yes; I saw them that time. But they are not people they are svartálfar or dark elves: creatures from the world of Svatalfaheimr. Vicious and cruel they are, but you don't see them often at all. They don't come out in daylight except at times of great need. Whatever that horn is, they are after it I would guess. Which means it must be important."

"Shall we ... just g-g-give it to them?" Hild asked in a shaky voice, "if they let us go, I m-m-mean."

Raedann shook his head. "They delight in causing harm and would not just let us go. They would take it and then kill us. We have to reach Gurthrunn."

The children gasped, staring with white, tense faces at Raedann. "Come on," he said, "keep up!"

He set off again, but as they ran on they saw more and more of the little dark figures, keeping pace with them on either side as well as following along behind. Anna saw one clearly only thirty paces away. He was smaller than a man, more like an older child. His skin was jet black, like the darkest of nights, but his teeth, which looked as sharp as needles, were a brilliant white. He ran along with his back slightly bent and his arms held out in front of him so that Anna could see the pointed talons on every finger. The creature saw Anna staring at him and snarled at her.

With the swarm of birds swooping and diving overhead and the svartálfar running along on each flank, Anna had the sudden feeling that they were fleeing along a tunnel or into a cave. As soon as she had the thought she realised why. The dark elves were not just pursuing them, they were channelling them: directing their flight where they wanted the children to go. But where, she asked herself, was that?

"Raedann they are letting us run. They are driving us somewhere."

The tinker nodded. "I know. Do you ..." he paused as he gasped for breath, "do you have your weapons?"

"We've each got a seax; Ellette has a sling and Lar a bow."

"Well we might need them now - look!" Raedann shouted as he stumbled to a halt.

Directly ahead of them lay a steep earthen bank - the base of the old hill fort. It was almost vertical at this point and impossible to climb. The svartálfar had brought them to a dead end. Now that they were cornered, the dark elves emerged from between the trees. Soon, Anna could count thirty of the creatures swarming towards them and as they scuttled forward they drew long, cruel-looking knives of curved black iron. Sharp and vicious weapons they were and Anna shivered in fear as she saw them.

As the six humans backed away towards the bank, all around them the dark elves' snarls changed into another noise. It started as a high pitched squeal and then it became what to Anna's ears sounded almost like ... laughter. Yes, it was; the creatures were laughing at them!

"Get behind me!" Raedann shouted as he turned to face the enemy. Drawing his long sword he gestured with it towards the approaching horde. The children huddled on either side of him: Anna stood next to him on his right, her seax at the ready. Lar stood beside her and placed an arrow on his bowstring. Ellette, on Raedann's left, had her sling out, and beyond her stood Wilburh.

The boy at first drew his seax, then put it away and fumbled in his pouch. In the blink of an eye he stood with his hands ready, holding in one clenched fist the iron symbol of Woden, father of the gods, and in the other a charm - a stick engraved with runes. He drew in a long breath and prepared to use sorcery. Hild, quaking and shivering, hunkered down behind Raedann. Yet frightened as she was, in one hand she held her seax and in the other her pouch of healing balms and potions.

Until this moment Anna had not really thought through what her wish to be a shield maiden actually meant. The night before, when those huge black dogs had chased them back to the ford, it all happened so quickly she barely had time to react, much less think it all over. Now though, it occurred to her that what she was feeling at this moment was exactly how she might feel if she did one day stand in a shield wall with her companions around her, weapon in her hand and a deadly enemy closing in upon them. Her heart was racing, pounding away in her chest like the hooves of a horse thundering across a meadow. Sweat was pouring from her forehead and dripping down her face, but oddly, her throat was bone dry so that she could hardly swallow.

"I'm frightened ..." she mumbled, turning to look at the travelling storyteller.

Raedann's gaze flickered briefly over her and she thought he was about to shout at her for being a scared little girl, but his reply surprised her.

"Good! So am I. It means you are not stupid. But to be afraid you must be alive. If you want to carry on living, keep hold of your seax and don't run. Here they come!"

He was right. The dark elves had closed to less than thirty paces away. Then their laughter changed to a roar and a moment later the svartálfar were charging.

"Use your bow!" Raedann shouted at Lar.

Lar hesitated and was obviously just as scared as Anna.

"Now boy - now!"

Drawing back his bow, Lar released his arrow. It sped across twenty paces and caught a dark elf in the shoulder, knocking the svartálfar off its feet and flinging it backwards into a gorse bush. There was a whirling noise from Anna's left and Ellette's sling-stone bounced off another elf's forehead and it collapsed unconscious on the ground.

"*Sunne- āblǣnden!*" Wilburh shouted. There was a flash of blazing light and three elves screamed in terror, blinded by the blast that hit them head on.

A second arrow left Lar's bow and another elf was hit - this time squarely in the chest. Watching it fall, Anna was certain it was dead. Then there was no time to think any more, for the svartálfar had arrived. One thrust a short spear towards Anna and she jumped to one side and then swung back with her seax. She felt her blade connect with the creature and heard it squeal in pain as it tumbled away from her. Another came on and its short sword clattered against her seax. The elf snarled at her and she could see its sharp teeth as it reached out to grab her neck. With their blades locked together she felt the claw-like hand tightening around her throat. Gasping for breath, she fought down a moment's panic then reacted in the only way possible. She kicked him - kicked as hard as she could. The elf snarled again, but this time in pain as it fell away from her.

Anna risked a glance around. On her right, Lar had backed off, giving him time to keep loading and shooting his bow, but she could see he had only two arrows left. 'Twang' went his bowstring and another elf was hit - but now Lar was down to his last arrow and there were six of the dark figures circling to his right, waiting for the last shot that would leave him defenceless. On her other side, Raedann was fighting a larger dark elf - perhaps the leader. Both had lost their swords and were grappling and wrestling with their bare hands. They fell onto the brambles at their feet and were now rolling under and over each other.

Wilburh was still waving his hands around, but seemed exhausted by his efforts. The magic had terrified the elves and they had kept back from him, but now they could see he was tiring and maybe did not have enough strength to repeat the spell. Finding their courage they came forward again. Five of them closed in on him, their curved knives at the ready.

Ellette had run out of stones and had drawn her seax, but as she prepared to fight with it, one of the elves ran at her and threw a javelin. It hit her in the arm and she screamed as she was knocked to the ground. Hild scuttled over to help her. A moment later it was Hild who screamed as a pair of evil-looking elves loomed over her, daggers ready to strike her down.

"What do we do?" Anna asked herself in despair. "I think we are about to die!"

CHAPTER NINE
THE FORT

The earth shook as a pair of heavy, iron-shod boots hit the ground next to Anna. Someone immensely strong and heavy had landed there. Looking upwards from the boots she could see that their owner was the dwarf, Gurthrunn. Seen up close like this Anna did not see him as short, though he was only about her height, but he looked incredibly strong. It was as if a wild bull had been thrust into a suit of chain mail designed for a twelve-year-old boy. The armour he wore bulged and stretched over a body that was just as muscular and powerful as a ferocious animal. His hands were clutched around a huge hammer, which resembled the symbol of the thunder god, Thunor.

He glanced down at Anna, nodded briefly at her then looked away and fixed the dark elves with a glare that carried no hint of mercy. Opening his mouth, he roared out a battle cry using words that Anna did not understand, and then he charged, swinging his hammer as he moved. It was a fearsome sight.

The hammer crashed into the chest of the nearest svartálfar and the creature was tossed like a doll far away into the forest. The reverse stroke smashed

another elf to the ground. The dwarf moved on through
the horde, bringing havoc and destruction.

Anna got to her feet, found her seax and began to follow Gurthrunn. She approached an elf who was cowering near an oak tree, his spear shaking and quivering as he watched the dwarven warrior advancing through the dark elves. Anna merely stepped towards him and with a screech of fear the elf was off, scampering away through the brambles.

An instant later the other elves were fleeing too. Gurthrunn's sudden arrival and furious assault had been too much for them and they were running through the trees screeching and screaming in terror. Gurthrunn crashed through the undergrowth in pursuit, roaring again as if calling the dark elves to turn and fight him. None would; they ran on even faster as he charged after them.

Moving over to Hild, Anna pulled her to her feet and then went to help Ellette, relieved to see that the little girl's arm wound was only a scratch and that nobody else was hurt. All of them, including Anna herself, were shocked by what had happened. They had heard stories of battles as told around the fire on a winter's night. Such tales were exciting and heroic, but they never mentioned how afraid the warriors were in a battle, nor how terrifying fighting could be.

Gurthrunn returned after a short while and stomped through the brambles towards the children. He came straight to Anna.

"Do you have the horn?" he asked without any

introduction or comment.

Finding that her throat was still too dry to speak, Anna simply nodded.

"Come!" he ordered and continued to march towards the fort, then turned and followed its base, making for the entrance away to the south. The children stared after him, each of them suddenly afraid of the mighty dwarven warrior.

"It is all right, you are safe," Raedann said as he saw their expressions.

"But ... but did you see what he d-d-did," Hild stuttered.

Raedann put a gentle hand on her shoulder. "What do you expect? Gurthrunn is a dweorg. He is not human, but take heart, child, he is a fearsome enemy of the dark elves and of those who set themselves against the Aesir - against the gods in Asgard. Long ago the gods trusted his race to create their greatest treasures - the Brisingamen of Freya, the hammer of Thunor and the spear of Woden, and many others. They do not merely forge the artefacts; they maintain a link to them. They will guard them ferociously. Or, when they feel that one has been misused or stolen, they will stop at nothing to recover it."

Anna's hand drifted to the horn at her belt and Raedann, seeing the gesture, nodded. "Yes, Anna, I mean the horn .... Come, let us follow him," he added with no further explanation.

Feeling suddenly dizzy, Anna swayed on her feet. If Raedann was right then the horn was not just a pretty object of value, but something that had been made for and used by the gods. So how had it got here and how had it ended up in the Roman villa? With these questions echoing through her head, she stumbled after the traveller, wondering what new secrets the day would bring.

Gurthrunn was waiting for them at the bottom of a path that led upwards into the fort. The fort itself was built up in three levels, each one smaller than the one below: concentric circles one on top of another. Raedann had told them that in those distant days when the old people lived here, the hillside would have been bare and from its heights an ancient chieftain could have looked out on the surrounding lands and watched an enemy army approach. Today, a forest had grown up around it and the trees hid much of the fortress. The fort's fences had long since rotted away leaving only mounds of earth, yet it was still steep-sided and the only easy way in was by the path. This cut through the first embankment and then circled the fort a quarter of the way round, before passing through another cutting on the east side of the second level.

Gurthrunn paused here and went over to the edge of the outer embankment to gaze down into the woodland. Anna realised he was looking at the spot where they had earlier fought the svartálfar and it must have been from this height that the dwarf had jumped to join them. It looked a long way down. The trees below were quiet and other than the bodies of the three dark elves they had killed in the battle, there was no sign of the enemy that had pursued them. Even the ravens seemed to have disappeared.

Gurthrunn grunted and without a word led them through the cutting and onward, making another quarter turn to the left, to a point high above where they had first entered the fort. A further gap in the embankment here provided a way into the third and final level.

Here there stood a small, round hut amongst the crumbled foundations of a dozen more. The single intact building had obviously been built in more recent times as the timbers did not show much sign of damage by rain or wind. Smoke spiralled skyward from an opening in the thatched roof. The dwarf opened the door and beckoned them to enter

The interior was gloomy and it took a few moments for Anna's eyes to adapt to the half light. A flame flared up over the embers of a fire in a pit on the other side of the room. Gurthrunn had lit a taper from the fire and now used it to ignite a candle lamp. He placed the lamp upon a table to the side of the hut and then gestured that they should all sit on benches on the opposite side.

"I forget just how poor human eyes are in the dark. We dweorgar prefer gloom to the bright light of day, but I know that your type likes light. Come, sit and we shall eat some roast fowl I caught earlier and drink a little mead."

The roast birds had been hanging over the embers cooking slowly all day, the dwarf told them, suddenly talkative despite his earlier gruffness. He cut the birds in half and handed a portion to each of them. As she bit into hers, Anna realised how hungry she was: they had not eaten all day. The meat was delicious. The mead that Gurthrunn poured into each of their drinking horns was just as sweet as the honey from which it was made. For a while the only noise was the slapping of lips, slurping of mead and contented groans.

"Now then," Gurthrunn said after they had eaten. "Let me just pop a couple of logs on the fire and then we can talk. You will be wanting to know about that horn I daresay."

Wiping her mouth with the back of her hand, Anna nodded, pulling the horn from her belt and examining it again in the flickering firelight.

"What is it? Raedann said it was made by your people for the ... well, the gods. Is that true?" she asked the dwarf.

His face illuminated by a faint golden glow from the horn, he nodded. "Yes. We made many such items in the days when the worlds were young and the gods young too. The gods desired the strength and the wisdom to govern and what we forged for them helped them in those tasks.

They loved the magical things we created and guarded the artefacts carefully. Yet there are those amongst them who are jealous, who would take from them all that they could: their lives and their power as well as their possessions. One of their own - the God Loki - has ever been envious of the other gods and has always worked to bring them down, stealing what he could and harming them. For his crimes Loki was imprisoned by Woden until the end of time, and yet he still interferes and plots and he has servants who would do his bidding and try to free him."

Gurthrunn got up and finding a stave used it to poke the fire into life. As the embers glowed and ash flew up into the air, he used the metal rod to point at the horn.

"That is the horn of the God Heimdall, the gatekeeper of the gods. With it one can open and close gateways between Asgard and Midgard. Indeed, it can open up the pathways between all of the Nine Worlds. That is a power all the treasures have, for that is how the gods are able to move amongst the stars when mere mortals cannot. Each treasure has its own unique power. The horn can also summon forth an army to fight at its wielder's command. As such it is a potent device and in the wrong hands would be devastating."

Anna's hands shook as she held the horn. It hardly seemed possible that it had been held by a god; that a god had put it to his lips and blown into it!

"What ... I mean, how did it get here?"

"That was Loki's doing. I told you that he has servants. He can be charming and persuasive when he wants to be and many beings have fallen under his spell. Many have been promised wealth and power if they will help him to overthrow the other gods. Mortals mostly, but immortals too: beings like Valkyries."

"The riders of the gods?" Wilburh said.

The dwarf nodded. "Indeed. Those that choose who will live and die in battle and then carry the souls of the slain to Valhalla to feast with Woden. That at least is what they are supposed to do. A noble task indeed. But some of the Valkyries were dissatisfied. Loki whispered in their ears and promised many things and some listened to him and agreed to serve him. One day they rode into Asgard and stole many of the precious items we had made for the gods. They took them and hid them amongst the Nine Worlds, ready for the day their master would use them."

"I don't imagine the gods were very happy about that," Raedann commented, his eyes bright with excitement as he listened to the tale. Anna could imagine he was making up a new story to tell on his journeys.

Gurthrunn shook his head solemnly. "No, they were not. Furious would be a fair word to describe them. A battle ensued between Loki and the gods. Loki lost and he and his followers were imprisoned deep in the dungeons of the underworld. But the items were still lost and Loki and his helpers refused to say where they were hidden."

The dwarf fell silent, gazing into the glowing embers of the fire. After a moment he continued, "Many items had been stolen, including the Brisingamen of Freya, Woden's spear, Thunor's hammer and the horn of Heimdall. The gods came to us - to the creators - for help, believing that since we had made the treasures we could perhaps track them down. We were tasked to locate the items and bring those who stole them to justice. That is what I am doing here in Midgard. It is the reason I am living in this hut."

"So the horn was brought here by one of Loki's followers?" Hild asked, hardly daring to look at the dwarf, of whom it seemed she was still afraid. "That is why you are here - to find it?"

Nodding, the dwarf pointed again at the horn. "One way that we track the treasures down is to listen to tales about magical items. I came across one such tale told in the taverns of Rome. It seems that when the Romans were living near here one of them went digging in an ancient barrow a few miles north of Scenestane. He wrote a letter about it to his brother back in Italy, saying that he had tried to open the sealed door to the barrow, but found that whatever he did he could not get it open. His tools would break and snap. He almost gave up, but then he came across a number of holes around the back of the barrow, probably dug out by a badger. Although the animal had long since gone, its sett had weakened the surface and there had been a cave-in. The Roman dug his way into the barrow from that side and found himself breaking into an underground chamber. In it he found precious coins and gems and ... a horn. It was a golden horn of great beauty. Yet when he blew it the Roman could not get any note from it. He took it home and everyone in his family had a go, but no one could get even a squeak out of it. He promised to bring the horn on a visit to his brother, but he never returned to Rome. The story goes that one day there was a terrible earthquake and the villa collapsed. Soon afterwards the Roman army in Britannia marched away to their wars and abandoned the country and so no one ever repaired the villa."

"But that was hundreds and hundreds of years ago," Anna remarked looking wide-eyed at the dwarf and wondering just how old he was.

"So you came here looking for a ruined villa?" Lar grinned, "Rather a lot of them about here aren't there?"

Gurthrunn grunted. "Indeed. So I discovered. I was beginning to search them one by one when to my surprise, last night I heard a sound clear across the valley. I knew that the horn had been found and it had been sounded. Now all I had to do was track it down."

"Several of us tried to play that horn," Ellette said peevishly, "but only Anna could get it to sound. Why was that?"

Gurthrunn fiddled with his beard as he seemed to ponder the question. "The horn is magical, child. We designed it to be used by gods and also by one type of person in moments of great need. A mortal might be able to get it to sound, might be able to use it, if they were the right type."

"What type?" they chorused.

"A champion: a leader of warriors in battle - a captain."

There was a sudden silence as they all stared at Anna. She looked around at their astonished faces then down at the horn and then back up again.

"Me?" she asked in a small voice.

CHAPTER TEN
VALKYRIE

"If you blew it, then a champion you are ... or might be one day. But you cannot keep the horn, child. It belongs to Heimdall and he will be wanting it back. We must make plans to achieve that before she tries again to take it from us."

"She ... you mean Kendra?" Anna asked absently, still a little dazed at being described as a champion.

Gurthrunn nodded.

"So who is she and why has she got the whole village acting so odd?" Hild asked.

"Odd? How odd?"

"Like they don't know us," Hild sobbed.

The dwarf raised his eyebrows at Anna, who told him what had happened, reporting the strange behaviour of the villagers, how even their own parents seemed not to recognise them and had chased after them, and how the men were engaged in very strange activities, all apparently at Kendra's command.

"Except for the children," she finished. "She does not seem to have much effect on the young ones and not on us either."

Gurthrunn listened carefully, fingering his warty face,

his expression grim. After Anna had spoken he was silent a moment, warming his hands on the fire. Then, drawing in a deep breath, he said, "I told you that Loki had talked many folk - mortal and immortal - into his service. Kendra is a Valkyrie - a warrior woman and servant of the gods, or leastways she was. What Loki promised her I do not know, but serve him she did - and does. It was she who stole two items of great power: the Brisingamen of Freya and the Horn of Heimdall. The Brisingamen is a necklace that emphasizes the powers of its mistress and Freya is the Goddess of Love and War. Her necklace makes the wearer strong and almost invincible in battle, but it also grants the ability to entrance mortals - and many immortals as well. Someone wearing it, who is strong enough, can turn men's hearts and those of women too, so that they adore the wearer and will do anything for them. Think, children, was Kendra wearing a necklace when you saw her?"

"Yes, she was and beautiful it was too," Ellette answered. "Do you think that was the Brisingamen?"

The dwarf nodded gravely. "I am afraid so. That is why your folk were behaving so oddly. Kendra has them all under her thrall. She is using the necklace to force them to her will. The Brisingamen only seems to work on adults. Apparently Freya ignores children when it comes to matters of war and love."

"It almost worked on me," Anna said in a small voice.

"Perhaps because you are almost no longer a child," Gurthrunn suggested.

Wilburh had been sitting very still listening to the dwarf, fascinated as he always was by tales of magic and the gods. He now asked a question.

"So, Kendra keeps the necklace with her. What about the horn? Why abandon it?"

"The horn she hid here so it would be ready for the day Loki would use it."

"Why not use it at once. Why wait?" Wilburh asked.

"I do not know the answer to that. Perhaps Woden led the gods against Loki before his plans were ready. Whatever the explanation, Kendra and Loki were captured by the gods and imprisoned over two hundred years ago. During that time my people have searched for the lost treasures and have found some, but the greatest has remained hidden from us. That might not have mattered until only a few days ago."

"Why? What happened?" Wilburh asked.

"Kendra, along with others in Loki's service, escaped from their prison. Heimdall immediately froze Bifrost - the bridge between the worlds - but not before Kendra was able to reach Midgard. She is here to find the treasures and once she does I do not know what she will do, but whatever it is, I must stop her."

"If she came looking for the horn where she hid it in the barrow she was out of luck. It was not there." Anna said.

Gurthrunn nodded. "Yes, she clearly believed it would be safe deep in a long abandoned burial mound, and so it might have been had our Roman not been curious two hundred years ago. Even then it was buried again until you found it in the villa and blew it. Had you not managed to get a sound out of it, neither she nor I would have been drawn to your little village."

"So what do we do? You talked about sending the horn back to Asgard. How is that possible?"

"There are paths and doors between the Nine Worlds if you know where to look, but it is not easy. Not these days. The gods have closed many of them in an attempt to stop their treasures being moved around and now that Kendra has escaped and Heimdall has frozen Bifrost, travel is even harder. Indeed, that very fact will make whatever Kendra is planning difficult. The gods let us dwarves travel in search of the artefacts, but without the gods' help it is not easy to pass between the worlds. The horn is the answer. It can open one of the doorways. It can give me access to Bifrost, the rainbow bridge that links Asgard to the other worlds."

"But what about Kendra? How do we deal with her? How do we free our parents from the spell that binds them?"

"I will help with that, but we must first get the horn away. If she gains control of it again she can summon an army to do her bidding. If that were to happen your people would be killed and your village burnt to the ground."

Her face paling at his words, Anna nodded. "So we get it away through one of these doorways. Where is it?"

"In the same barrow where you found the horn. The

entrance will act as my gateway. Such places have immense power for they are places where folk once passed from life to death. The doorway will give me access to Bifrost."

Raedann got up and went over to the hut door, opened it a fraction and glanced outside. "It is almost dark. We should not travel during the night," he suggested.

"No indeed," Gurthrunn shook his head. "Those svartálfar like darkness. If we were to get caught outside before dawn we would be in trouble even with me accompanying you."

"Why are the dark elves attacking us? And what about those horrid ravens?" Hild asked.

"Kendra has the svartálfar that live here under her thrall. The Brisingamen would work on them just like it does on humans, but in their case they were drawn to Loki's side and will help Kendra to free him. As for the ravens – well, they serve the Valkyries, they fly with them when they go to battles and scout for them."

A thought occurred to Anna. "Won't the svartálfar attack us here?"

"Not right away. Their defeat today will give them pause for thought. The dark elves are nasty little creatures but they are easily frightened. They will have run away. It will take time for Kendra's ravens to find them again and still more time to persuade them to attack. Besides, I have cast certain spells of protective magic here. This place is safe for a while at least."

Gurthrunn stood and opened up a chest in the corner of his hut. When he turned back to the children he was carrying an armful of blankets. Handing one to each child he indicated that they should find a space on the floor to lie down. "Come, let us sleep and be about our business when the sun rises," he ordered. "I will keep watch over you tonight." So saying, he carried his great hammer towards the door.

The children settled down for the night and soon Anna could hear first Raedann, then Wilburh and Lar snoring. She looked around at the girls and found that they were also asleep. But sleep did not come easily to her. In her mind she saw herself once more blowing the horn and remembered how she had felt: the strange exhilaration that had run through her; a power she had not felt before. Then that image was gone and with terrifying clarity she recalled the battle below the fort in the forest. She had been so scared. Hardly a champion; hardly a leader of warriors or a captain!

The arguments she had with her father were always about her dreams of becoming a shield maiden, a warrior woman destined to fight the enemies of her people. Now, having been in battle today for real, she realised how uncertain she was about those dreams.

After what seemed a long time of tossing and turning,

Anna got up and throwing the blanket around her shoulders like a cloak, she quietly opened the door and stepped out into the night. Gurthrunn was sitting near a fire he had built not far from the door. He looked up at her, an unspoken question in his eyes as she joined him on a log near the fire.

"I can't sleep," she said.

At first Gurthrunn said nothing, but studied her from under his bushy eyebrows then said, "You have something on your mind, mayhap? Something to do with what I said tonight?"

She nodded. "I was frightened today. When the dark elves attacked us I thought we were going to die and I was scared."

"I imagine you were. Any sane person would be, child. Battles are terrible places. A warrior knows fear in his or her heart, but fights despite it. Fights because of it perhaps, because fear reminds you that you are mortal and can die and you don't want to die, and you don't want those you care for to die either. So you fight to live that they may live also."

Anna realised that the horn was in her hand again. She had taken it out of her belt when she was listening to Gurthrunn. "This horn - you say it can only be blown by a champion - a leader in battle. Before tonight I wanted to be one, but after that battle I am not so sure. I am not sure

I can be."

"What you are and what you can be is your wyrd - your fate. Trust in your fate. It will not lead you astray. If destiny decrees that you will be a warrior, so you shall be. The horn could feel that in you: something about you that the others do not have. You are destined to lead and they to follow. Like all the treasures of the gods, the horn looks for rare people like you. It feels in you just a touch of the power that the gods have. That is why only you could get it to sound."

"So you are saying I must believe in my wyrd. I must trust in my destiny?" Anna asked, still far from certain she was convinced.

Gurthrunn nodded.

"Indeed, that is all any of us can do. Now go and try to sleep, child. The morning will be upon us ere long. "

CHAPTER ELEVEN
BARROW

The following morning was grey and a cold wind blew across the top of the fort. Gurthrunn gave them each some bread to break their fast and when they had eaten they prepared to depart.

"Do you want to carry the horn, Gurthrunn?" Anna asked the dwarf as they followed the path back down to the forest below. She reached for the horn at her belt and held it out to him.

Gurthrunn shook his head. "Not until I am ready to pass through the door and cross Bifrost. The artefacts are relatively dormant in the hands of mortal men - unless in the case of the horn you were to blow it, of course - but we dwarves have magic in our very bones. If I was to touch it, it would awaken and Kendra would feel that from afar. It would be best not to give her warning of where we are. You carry it and keep it safe."

Anna nodded and tucked the treasure away, then a thought occurred to her. "Will it not already be awakened? When I blew it I mean?"

"Certainly Kendra will have felt that moment. It is what drew her to your village. But to wake fully, each of the treasures must first join with the person who uses it and choose him or her to be its wielder. Then at the will of the bearer the full powers of the treasure are awoken."

'Chosen' - the word came back to Anna like an echo of the first time she had heard it. "Gurthrunn, when I blew the horn it said - leastways I think it said - the word 'chosen.'"

The dwarf halted and turned to stare at her, "Really?"

"Yes, we all heard it. Sorry, we forgot to mention it. Was it important?"

"You could say that," Gurthrunn chuckled. "I will have to ponder this a while. Come, let us press on."

Wanting to avoid the village as much as possible, the route Gurthrunn took led them first north through the woods towards Watling Street. Throughout the morning they were able to keep under cover of the trees and saw no sign of raven or svartálfar. When they had been walking for quite a while, Anna noticed that Raedann and Gurthrunn were speaking quietly together as they wandered along side by side. Curious, she drifted closer, hoping to overhear what they were saying, but whatever it was, they had stopped by the time she was near enough to hear.

They broke their journey at the edge of the forest and ate some cheese and smoked meats that Gurthrunn had brought from his hut. The dwarf then left them to finish their food and scouted ahead on the planned route for the afternoon. While he was gone, Anna caught a movement in the corner of her vision. Glancing up she was just quick enough to see the shape of a large, black-feathered bird flapping away from its perch at the top of a nearby beech tree and vanishing into the sky. It gave her a creepy feeling and she was about to mention it, when she became aware that Lar and Raedann were peering at her with evident curiosity as they sat chatting quietly on the other side of the little dell. She knew they were talking about her.

"What is it?" she asked, forgetting the bird, her patience at being stared at finally running out.

"Nothing," Lar answered a bit too quickly and she knew her brother was lying. She gave him a long stare. He stared back for a moment then blushed and looked away. "It's been two years since Ma died," he mumbled, "but when you glare at me like that you remind me of her."

"Yes, I know," she replied sadly. "Just like me, she could tell when you were lying, Lar Nerianson, so go on - tell me what you were talking about and why you were staring at me."

Lar sighed. "The horn. Raedann and I were just saying that it is a shame we have to send it away - that's all."

"Oh, I suppose you would rather sell it then?"

"Of course we would rather sell it. Have you looked at it? Worth a lot that is; more than you imagine, I would say. We could be rich!"

"I don't think Gurthrunn would take well to you selling Heimdall's horn," Wilburh muttered. "I expect the gods would also react badly to such a trade."

Anna was about to agree with Wilburh, a hot retort on her lips directed at Lar, but at that moment Gurthrunn returned through the thicket to the east of the dell. Glancing round at the suddenly silent party, he raised a warty eyebrow and then just barked out an order in his gruff voice. "Come, the land is clear. We can reach the barrow by mid-afternoon if we go quickly."

As they left the woodlands behind, and passed into the open north of Scenestane, the grey skies that had loomed overhead all morning grew blacker and the wind picked up. Soon afterwards it started raining. Although gentle at first, the rain became increasingly heavy and by the time they crossed the Roman road a couple of miles north of the villa, it was torrential. Soaked to the skin, they pressed on across the fields, which were now becoming a quagmire. Their feet sank into the soft, wet ground and lumps of thick mud clung to the girls' and Raedann's sandals, the boys' shoes and Gurthrunn's boots, making them heavier and heavier.

"Blast the weather!" Raedann muttered. "Just our luck that it should choose today to change to rain."

Gurthrunn grunted. "If it is luck," he commented.

"What do you mean?" Anna asked.

"I mean this mud is slowing us down. I would not put it past Kendra to use some sorcery to manipulate the weather. Valkyries can influence the winds and the Brisingamen would enhance any powers the wearer had. "

"How does she know where we are though?" Wilburh asked.

"Er ... I think I saw a bird when we stopped to eat. I'm not sure, but it might have been a raven," Anna said, suddenly recalling the bird. "I meant to mention it, but ..." her voice trailed away and she scowled at Lar.

"Well, if you did see one, Kendra might be tracking us. Come, we must press on, we are only a mile away," Gurthrunn ordered.

As they walked on, the rain became lighter and soon stopped completely. The afternoon sun broke through the cover of clouds and for the first time since setting off that morning they felt its warmth on their backs.

"Praise the gods for that!" Lar commented.

"Don't be so pleased. Look!" Ellette shouted.

They all glanced in the direction she was pointing. A small stand of oak trees grew out of a mound in the ground away to the south. At first they could not see what was bothering her and Ellette, whose eyes were sharpest, pointed again at the very top of one of the trees. Perched there, watching them with its head cocked to one side, was a single, large raven. It opened its beak, crowed at them and then, with a flap of wings, was aloft and soaring away.

Despite the welcome warmth of the sun, Anna

shivered, "How far now, Gurthrunn?"

"Not far - look now," he pointed, "you can just see the barrow not far from Watling Street."

They hurried on towards the mound that was visible a few hundred paces away. It stood in the middle of a wide expanse of short grass between two stretches of woodland. As they came closer they could see that the mound, which was about seventy paces long and thirty wide, was covered in the same short grass. The end they were approaching was the one with the door. Cut into the mound at this end was a narrow channel leading to a stone archway, but this was blocked in the centre by a huge stone slab, which sealed the way inside. From a distance Anna could make out the lines of runes etched into the stonework of the archway. The children scurried along behind Gurthrunn across the last stretch of grassland before the tomb.

"Look there!" Ellette shouted, pointing at the doorway. Above it, talons wrapped around the lintel, was the raven.

"We must hurry," the dwarf shouted, "she will be coming!" None of the children felt the need to ask to which 'she' Gurthrunn referred.

"Drive it away!" he ordered and Ellette, quick to pull out her sling, whirled it around her head and flung a stone at the bird. The stone clattered into the lintel between the raven's feet. Startled, the creature screeched and launched itself into flight, swinging low over their heads and then wheeling away.

The dwarf grunted his approval and then stomped over to the doorway. He studied it for a moment then placed one hand on each of the upright stones that supported the lintel, one on either side of the doorway. His eyes now closed, he began to mutter an incantation - a spell.

Anna did not recognise the words; they were not English, nor Welsh, which she had heard occasionally from traders visiting the village, but some other language. Perhaps it was Dweorgar. The sound was like thunder rumbling towards you from a distant storm, or the hoofbeats of a horse galloping down a road. Hearing it, Anna felt as if the earth was moving beneath her feet, as if the words could force stone and soil to obey them. Yet, after a moment Gurthrunn stepped back and shook his head.

"Normally we dwarves can open Bifrost, for we helped to construct it with our blood and sweat. I thought therefore to give it a try, but it is no good, this gateway is firmly shut. I will need the horn to persuade it to yield to my command." Turning to Anna, he held out is hand, "Anna, pl ...."

He was interrupted by a sudden shout of rage coming from the nearby woods. Anna thought at first it was the bird, but when she looked up she saw that gathered under the trees was the entire adult population of the village: thirty people, each armed with a weapon. Some carried spears and axes, some only a short sword - a seax like Anna's own. Others clutched tools: the billhooks, picks and shovels they used around the village. Dotted amongst the villagers were the dark elves that had battled with Anna and her companions the previous day.

The elves and humans just stood there watching the children, then they moved apart and suddenly Kendra was standing in the midst of them.

The sorceress walked forward to confront Gurthrunn. "Dweorg, this is not your world," she hissed.

"Neither is it yours, traitor, but I at least am here at the bidding of the gods."

"The gods are weak and will fall. My master will rule and I will be his queen."

Gurthrunn grunted. "Ah, so that is what he promised you to persuade you to betray them. I wonder how many others he has promised the same or similar. Loki, the trickster god: do you really trust him?"

"Give me the horn!" Kendra yelled, ignoring the question.

"Never!"

Kendra's face twisted into a mask of rage. She nodded her head as if a decision had been made. "Very well, then. You shall die and these children along with you." Pointing her long finger at Anna nd her friends she shouted back to the villagers.

"Attack them!"

chapter twelve
the horn is lost

The villagers moved out of the woods and spread out as they approached. Passing Kendra, they lifted their weapons, preparing to use them ... preparing to cut down their own children where they stood.

Anna felt a chill travelling up her spine. Somehow this was far worse than when the svartálfar alone had attacked. They at least were the enemy. This time their attackers were not just creatures they did not know. These were also their mothers and fathers, their uncles and aunts. Scenestane was not a large village and everyone knew everyone else. The adults were normally very protective of their children. At least Anna had always found it so. But today it was quite different. As the people she knew and loved moved towards them, threatening them with spear, scythe, sword and axe, their faces showed no concern. It was if the children were a strip of wheat they were coming to cut down.

The warrior dwarf had his hammer in his hand now and was raising it ready to bring it crashing down on Meccus, who was in the lead, but Anna stopped him.

"No, Gurthrunn!" she shouted, shaking her head. "We cannot fight them. Not our parents."

"Can't we just run?" Ellette asked, her sharp eyes searching for an escape route, but it was obvious that they would not get far before being hunted down.

"What are we going to do?" Hild cried. The villagers were surrounding them now, forming a ring around the children - a ring that was closing in upon them.

"Give me the horn," Gurthrunn said.

"Are you sure? Last night you said ..."

"Never mind what I said. It is too late. We cannot get away. Give me the horn."

Anna pulled the horn out of her belt and passed it to the dwarf.

He held it up high. "Stop!" he bellowed in a voice full of authority. "Here is the horn, Kendra - come and take it from me."

"Halt!" Kendra's equally loud command was shouted from behind the villagers. A moment later she roughly pushed her way between Nerian and Iden. Her eyes widened when she saw the horn in the dwarf's hand. In two bounds she was in front of him.

"Please give that to me," she said, but now her tone was no longer harsh, instead it was soft and beautiful, the voice that had charmed an entire village now being used to try to charm one dwarf.

Gurthrunn laughed. "My Lady, we made that necklace you are wearing. Do you really think I would be vulnerable to its effects? But I will give the horn to you if you will spare the lives of the children."

Kendra studied Gurthrunn for a moment and then nodded, turning to bark out an order at the villagers. "Put away your weapons. Seize the children and this other man," she pointed at Raedann, "but do not harm any of them. Take them to the temple and tie them up."

Anna felt a pair of heavy hands slap down onto her shoulders and the next moment she was twisted around so quickly she felt dizzy. She looked up to see that the man holding her was none other than her own father.

"Papa - it's me, Anna. Anna your daughter!"

Nerian did not respond. He pulled her hands together and looped some rope around them and then tugged to tighten the knot. The cord dug into her wrists and pinched her skin.

"Ouch, Father - you're hurting me!"

Nerian looked straight into her eyes and Anna felt her heart sink. There was not even a glimmer of recognition. It was as if he did know who she was – or if he did, he did not care.

"Come," he ordered and pulling at the rope led her towards Scenestane. Around her the other children and Raedann were also being led along. Each of them tied up, miserable, scared and bewildered. Capture was frightening enough, but it was the fact that their families, the people who normally loved and protected them, yet who were now treating them so roughly and ignoring their pleas, that really hurt and scared them.

"Father, please!" Anna tried again.

"It will do no good," Raedann said. He was also being dragged along, the blacksmith tugging at the rope that bound him. "They are under her influence and do not know what they do. We must look for a chance to escape."

"What is the point? She has the horn. She has won," Lar muttered.

The villagers dragged them up the hill to the wooded glade and then pushed them into the temple. The door was slammed shut behind them and they were left in the gloomy interior. The single candle left burning on the altar their only light.

"Everyone all right?" Hild asked as they dragged themselves onto their feet.

"Sure," said Lar, "but what do we do now?"

"Well, I do have a plan," Raedann replied.

Anna, feeling confused, was in no mood to hear it. "Why did Gurthrunn give Kendra the horn? He didn't even try to escape. Maybe he too is under her spell. He could have used the horn and summoned an army after all," she said, throwing herself onto one of the benches.

"Not without harming someone from the village. That was on his mind," Raedann answered.

"You said it yourself, Anna," Hild reminded her. "If there had been a battle, someone would have got hurt." The younger girl was sitting with her back against the altar, nibbling at the knot that tied her hands together.

"Most likely our own people," Ellette commented, looking thoughtful as she examined her own bindings.

"There was another reason he did not use the horn," Raedann said.

"What was that?" Wilburh asked.

"Because he could not."

"What?" Anna asked.

Raedann scratched his head as if he was deciding whether or not to say something important. In the end he looked up at Anna. "It was because of you, child," he said.

"What?" Anna's eyes widened. "Me?"

"Yes, you." Raedann was walking around the room now. "Earlier today Gurthrunn told me he suspected that something remarkable had happened to the horn. Like all the treasures the dwarves created for the gods, the horn has a special ability. It was designed to look for the most appropriate person to match its special powers. Thunor's hammer would look for the strongest being to wield it; Woden's spear for the wisest creature, and so on. The idea was that when the artefacts were given to the gods they would naturally bind with them and the pair - god and treasure - would act as one. But what neither the dwarves nor the gods seemed to predict was that the treasures, because of the way they were made, have a need to belong. It is in their very nature. They need a master or mistress to use them."

"So?" Wilburh asked.

"Just imagine for a moment that the worst thing happened. Let's say that - the gods forbid - your parents died and you were left alone, orphaned and with no one to look after you. In that situation what do you suppose would be your wish? What would you desire above all things?" Raedann asked, his gaze moving over each of them.

The children looked at one another, uncertain how to answer, until Ellette responded. Her usual bright voice was subdued. "I would look for someone else to look after me."

Raedann beamed. "Ellette you are a genius!"

The little girl grinned. "I know, but no one else realises it."

Winking at her, Raedann turned to the others. "The little elf is right. You would try to find someone else to care for you. It's the human thing to do and, as it turns out, it's also the way the treasures of the gods think too. Since they need to belong, they are looking for someone to own them, someone to wield them. Yet, it is not just anyone. The owner must be the right person. They must have the abilities the treasures desire. They must be," he paused and looked at Anna, "chosen by the item."

"Chosen? That is what the horn said when I blew it," Anna gasped.

"Yes. Just so," Raedann answered with a nod, and

then said no more.

There was a stunned silence. Anna became aware that everyone in the dark temple was staring at her. "M-m-me?" she stuttered in a weak voice.

"Yes, Anna. The horn has chosen you. It was bonded to Heimdall and belonged to him for the untold aeons since it was created. Then it was stolen and hidden by Kendra. It was abandoned alone in the darkness, first in the barrow for who knows how long and then in the villa for another two hundred years. It was looking for a new master or mistress: a champion; a leader of warriors in battle; a captain. Two days ago, it found her – you!"

Anna did know what to say. She just stared at the bard, dumbfounded.

"Even if what you say is true," Lar said, "it does not explain why Gurthrunn could not use the horn, either to open the gate to Asgard or to summon an army."

"Oh, yes it does," Wilburh answered. "The horn is now bonded to Anna. It cannot be used by anyone else. Not unless she releases it or ..." he stumbled to a halt, turning to stare at her.

"Or what?" Anna asked dreading the answer.

"Or you are killed."

The temple door was flung open and standing outside were four of the villagers illuminated by a torch held high by Nerian.

"You, girl - come with me," her father said, barking out the order.

"What, why?" Barely able to speak for fear, she cringed away from the man her father had seemingly become. He seemed more like a stranger to her now than ever before.

"Kendra has asked to see you. At once!"

CHAPTER THIRTEEN
THE HORN IS STOLEN

"She is not going!" Lar said, jumping to his feet and moving to stand between Anna and their father. Nerian gave him the briefest of glances and then without any warning lashed out, his hand catching Lar across the face and sending him tumbling, blood dripping from his mouth, into Wilburh.

"Father!" Anna shouted, "That was Lar! Your son."

Nerian did not respond. He took two steps into the room, seized hold of her arms and dragged her towards the door. Once they were outside, one of the villagers slammed the door and barred it.

"Papa, you are hurting me," Anna complained, feeling Nerian squeezing her arm tightly.

"Come!" he replied, and tugging at Anna, pulled her along towards the path that led down into the village.

"Father you are being controlled. You are under a spell!" Anna cried out as she fought against his powerful grip. It was no use though - he was just too strong. She tried talking to him again, but it was clear that he was completely under Kendra's influence.

"Please!" she tried again. "It's her necklace, Papa, it's the Brisingamen - she is using it to control you. We have to get it off her!"

It was useless and giving up, Anna allowed herself to be taken across the village to the headman's hall and pushed inside.

The fire in the hall was roaring and she could feel its heat even from the doorway. All around the firepit about twenty-five dark elves were sitting or standing, cruel grins on their faces as they watched what was happening to Gurthrunn, who was kneeling in front of the fire, his hands bound behind him. His face was red and swollen, and covered in cuts and bruises. Meccus was standing in front of the dwarf and from the blood on the blacksmith's hands it was clear he was the one who had been striking Gurthrunn.

"Again!" screeched Kendra and Anna could see her now, sitting at a bench behind Meccus. The big man swung his fist and it connected with the dwarf's chin sending him tumbling onto his back. The dark elves cackled and howled in joy at the sight.

Kendra walked across the hall and stood looking down at the battered figure at her feet. "Tell me how to control the horn, dweorgar, or you and the children will all die."

"No!" Gurthrunn replied.

At this moment, Nerian shoved Anna in the back. Pushed forward into the circle of light created by the fire she stumbled down onto her knees.

"Very well," Kendra said, looking up and fixing the girl with a gaze that terrified her. "Perhaps there is someone here who will."

Anna had seen Kendra when she arrived in the village, heard her speak at the barrow, but this was the first time she had been the centre of the woman's attention. Although Anna had been told by Gurthrunn that Kendra was a Valkyrie, it was only now at this moment, when Kendra stepped forward to stand over her, that Anna became fully aware that this being was not human. There was something in her stance, something in the power she projected and something in her gaze that carried with it a sense of immortality. This was a creature that had lived whilst untold generations of mankind were born and died. She had seen a thousand wars fought, won and lost, and she had carried the souls of ten thousand fallen warriors to Valhalla. She had witnessed incredible courage by mortal men on a thousand battlefields and yet ... she did not care. She did not see in mankind their courage and honour, but dismissed them as petty creatures whose brief lives were meaningless when compared to her own and those of the gods. Looking up at the tall creature that projected herself as a beautiful woman, Anna, in a moment of stark clarity, realised that this was the problem with the being that stood in front of her.

'We humans appreciate courage, love, honour and

sacrifice, for without them we are just animals. Kendra is a Valkyrie and should know all this,' thought Anna, remembering all that she had been told about them, mostly by Raedann. The stories said that Valkyries looked for courage and bravery, rewarding those who demonstrated it with life eternal amongst the gods. But not this one! If Kendra had ever had those feelings she had long since lost them. This Valkyrie wanted only one thing: power. The god Loki had promised it to her and the triumph in her eyes suggested that today she was one step closer to achieving it.

Then, as Kendra looked down upon her, Anna's mind went blank and she felt suddenly ashamed at thinking such nasty thoughts about this wondrous being. She shook her head and reminded herself that Kendra was beautiful, kind and wise. Indeed, she could not understand why she had ever felt differently. She smiled up at the Valkyrie, feeling suddenly calm and no longer afraid.

"Tell me," Kendra said in a soft voice, which for some reason reminded Anna of how wonderful it feels to awaken on a warm summer's day with little to do but play in the woods and meadows until evening meal time.

Leaning forward, Kendra pulled out her knife and sliced through the rope binding Anna's wrists. "There you are, is that better?" she smiled. "Now then, Anna dear, tell me, what do you know of the horn?" Kendra turned and gestured towards the horn, which Anna could now see sitting on a table near the back of the hall where the door to the kitchens was located.

An immense desire to say the right thing came over Anna and she wanted to tell Kendra everything - how they had found the horn; that she had blown it and how they knew she was bound to it. She knew the Valkyrie might kill her to get control of the horn, but she did not care. Nothing mattered except pleasing Kendra. Anna was just opening her mouth to speak, when suddenly she heard a whispered voice speaking to her.

"Do not tell her, Anna. She is not my Mistress, you are!"

Anna turned her head to see where the voice was coming from, but there was only Nerian standing there and this voice was certainly not his. This voice was more musical, as if someone was singing softly rather than speaking. Nobody else seemed to have heard it.

"What?" Anna asked, terribly confused. All of a sudden, her calm acceptance of a moment ago fractured back into fear.

"Tell me, about the horn, child!" Kendra's tone was not as soft, not quite as charming as before; a touch irritated even.

"Do not tell her. Trust me. All is well," the sing-song voice repeated.

"Tell me!" Kendra shouted and this time there was just

anger. She seized Anna by the arms and shook her.

Wriggling in the Valkyrie's grasp, her head being shaken back and forth, Anna saw a sudden movement out of the corner of her eye. Then she spotted Ellette sneaking into the hall from the kitchen door. The little girl was hiding from Kendra and the dark elves by ducking behind one of the wooden posts that held up the roof. Anna was bewildered to see her there. Somehow the little girl had got free and escaped the temple. How had she managed it and what about the others? Then Anna remembered the small opening in the wall. Agile Ellette must have slipped out of her bonds and then squeezed out of their old escape route, which meant she was probably on her own for the others were too big to get through the gap.

Ellette's tense little face was filled with alarm when she saw what was happening to Gurthrunn and Anna. Edging out from the post, her hand came up holding a knife from the kitchen.

Anna had to think quickly. It would do no good for Ellette to attack on her own, brave as she was. Out of Kendra's sight, Anna mouthed the word 'No!' and tilted her head towards the table upon which the horn lay. The little girl spotted it, nodded and dropped to her knees to crawl unseen behind the table. So far so good; yet if Ellette reached out to grab the horn now, one of the elves might spot the movement. Anna knew she needed to create a distraction. Still struggling against the Valkyrie's strong hands, she shouted, "Wait - wait! I will help you."

Although her shout was directed at Kendra, Anna hoped that Ellette would understand the hidden message and delay her planned theft a short while.

Kendra relaxed her grip and smiling in triumph stepped back for a moment. And a moment was all Anna needed. She leapt to her feet and ran towards the door. She did not get far. Nerian jumped after her, his strong arms wrapped around her and threw her back into the hall. Two svartálfar seized her and pulled her back to face Kendra.

"Foolish girl! What did you do that for?" Kendra shouted as Anna was tossed onto her knees before the Valkyrie. Chancing a glance over to the horn Anna was relieved to see that it had vanished. She spotted Ellette scampering out of the door just before Kendra moved forward blocking the view. Everyone's gaze was fastened on Kendra and Anna and nobody else had seen little elf. Hiding a smile, Anna looked down at the floor.

The Valkyrie was clearly angry, but also a little surprised that Anna was not under the spell any more. Her eyes narrowed dangerously as she stepped closer to the girl. "This is your last chance. I know that the horn has bonded with someone and not this dweorgar. You carried the horn. You handed it to him when we caught you. You are the oldest of the children and their leader in games and sport according to the villagers. But games are over, child. I need the horn released to me. You have resisted my powers - the powers of this," Kendra said, fingering the Brisingamen that hung about her neck. "This is how I know you are bound to the horn. Only the powers of one of the gods' artefacts could shield a mortal from that of another. You are linked to the horn and it has freed you from my power.

"Now - enough delay. You must release the horn to me. This dwarf will not tell me how that would be done. So you can tell me. You can release the horn and then I will command it."

"I ... I don't know how."

"You lie child!" Kendra screamed and reaching to her belt drew a long curved dagger from it and held the blade at Anna's throat.

"Tell me what you know!"

Anna was terrified, but she wanted to give Ellette time to get away so had to keep Kendra talking. "Even if I did know - why would I tell you? You have cast a charm over my village so that my people are no better than slaves to you. You have hurt us and threatened our lives. I want you away from here, Kendra. That is my price. I will tell you what I know if you leave."

"I agree - now tell me," the Valkyrie snapped without hesitation.

"Not here and not now," Anna shook her head. "I will go with you, away from here. You will free my people and when I can see they are free then I will tell you."

Gurthrunn lifted his bloodied head and spoke. "No child! You cannot trust her."

"Silence dweorgar!" Kendra shouted at the dwarf and then, as Anna had been dreading she would, she turned to get the horn and spotted it was not there.

"How ...?" The woman gasped. In a flash the knife was back at Anna's throat. Around the hall the svartálfar cackled and hissed in anticipation of the spilling of a human's blood.

Kendra's eyes were bright with a fierceness that made Anna feel cold despite the nearby flames. The Valkyrie moved her hand forward and the girl could feel the blade's sharp edge nick her skin, a trickle of blood warm on her neck.

"Tell me where the horn is or I will kill you this instant!"

CHAPTER FOURTEEN
RAEDANN ESCAPES

As the blade pressed closer to her windpipe Anna realised that Kendra would do it – this was not a game. The Valkyrie would cut her throat without a second thought. Then the horn would be released and maybe Kendra would be chosen as its new mistress and would take on its powers, summoning an army to conquer Mercia, then Angleland and then maybe all of Midgard. She would reign supreme over the whole world!

It seemed at that moment the Valkyrie had come to the same conclusion, for Kendra's eyes shone with sudden thought. "You know what I think, mortal child? I think that I do not need any clever magic to give me control of the horn. There is no enchantment necessary to free it from bondage to you. Thy life and thy blood would be sufficient. All I must do is slay thee and my troubles will be over."

Anna hardly dared to breathe for fear of the steel blade that pressed at her neck, but she knew that she had to say something. "What if you are wrong? What if killing me does not work? Maybe you will never control the horn. Dare you take that risk?"

A flicker of doubt showed in Kendra's eyes and she hesitated, pulling back slightly, the pressure on the sharp edge of the blade just a fraction less. This moment's pause saved Anna's life, for just then the door to the headman's hall burst open and Iden the priest hurried into the room, puffing and panting and almost hopping from foot to foot in excitement. Kendra looked up with irritation at the man.

"Well? What is it?" she asked, her blade still held against Anna's throat.

"My Lady Kendra, come quickly!"

"Why? Can't you see I am busy?"

"It's Raedann, Mistress, he was seen escaping the village just now."

"That filthy tinker? He hardly matters does he?"

"The horn, though ..." Iden's voice trailed away to silence as his mistress looked sharply at him.

"What about the horn, priest?" Kendra snapped, stepping back from Anna and removing the blade.

Anna's throat stung. She rubbed her hand across it and felt blood sticky on her fingers. Kendra ignored her, all her attention now focused on the fat little priest.

"Well?"

"Raedann has it! He managed to escape from the temple and overpower Aelwulf the miller who was guarding the door. I was too far away to stop him, but I heard one of the children shouting after the tinker to bring the horn back and not to sell it."

Anna glanced across at Gurthrunn. What had happened?

It was clear that having stolen the horn Ellette had given it to the story teller. She must have helped him to escape from the temple? But how had they avoided the guards? And had Lar persuaded Raedann that they should try to sell the horn after all? Seeing the angry expression that flashed over Gurthrunn's face, Anna wondered if he was having the same thought.

"Raedann is a trader and tinker as you say, Mistress," Nerian commented. "If he has the horn he may try to reach Tamwerth with it and sell it at the market there. Many in the King's court would pay a high price for such a treasure."

Kendra's face went red with fury. "Find him! Get the whole village on the hunt. Now Nerian! At once! Get after him. Search the road; search the woods, search every farm. Leave not a stone unturned and when you find him, kill him and bring me the horn!"

Nerian nodded and moved towards the door, then hesitated and pointed at Anna and Gurthrunn. "What of these two, Mistress. Shall I kill them?"

Anna cried out in horror at his words and the matter of fact way he spoke them. Her own father! He barely even looked at her. There was no love or affection in his voice; just cold-hearted obedience to his mistress. "Papa ...' she let out a whispered sob, her throat aching, the image of her father blurring as tears filled her eyes.

Kendra studied Anna and the dwarf for a moment before making a decision. "No," she said at last. "They may still be of use. Take them and the other children and move them to a secure place. Clearly there is some other way out of the temple. Ensure they are well bound and guarded and then get on with the hunt. The svartálfar will remain to protect me. Now, obey me, Nerian!"

"At once, Mistress."

Once again seized by her father, her wrists tied even more tightly than before, Anna was dragged out of the hall. Nerian and two other villagers took her and Gurthrunn and this time led them both to the village store where the stocks of food were kept. This was a large hut that leant against the rear wall of the headman's hall and had only one way in: a heavy wooden door that was sealed with an iron lock to prevent theft when times were lean and food had to be rationed. At harvest time fruit and vegetables were laid carefully between layers of straw, or boiled and preserved in pots sealed with honey and wax before being stacked on the shelves. When pigs, sheep and cows were killed in the autumn, their carcases were smoked or salted and hung from hooks fixed into the roof. Cheeses wrapped in cloth were stored here too, along with ale and wine in clay jars. Anna had always found the smells in the storeroom to be quite wonderful and mouth-watering.

"Well," Gurthrunn grunted between swollen lips, one eye half shut, his face rapidly turning black and blue, "at least we won't starve."

"Give me your keys!" Nerian ordered Anna.

When Anna's mother had been alive she had carried the keys to the store, as was her right and duty as wife to the headman. That duty had fallen to his daughter, who, once the novelty had worn off, had found counting pots of food and making sure they had enough grain for the winter rather dull.

Anna reached down and fumbled with the set of iron keys at her belt. It was hard with her hands bound and Nerian's growing impatience made it even harder, but at last she got them free. Handing the keys over, Anna gazed into his eyes in the hope of seeing a flicker of remorse. But there was nothing; he was like a stranger.

Moments later the other four children, their hands bound, were herded into the store and the door slammed shut. They could hear the key scraping in the lock and they were left alone in the dark, their only light that which filtered through the thatched roof or under the door.

Waiting until her eyes adjusted to the gloom, Anna turned to Lar. "What did you do? I already figured out that Ellette managed to wriggle free of her bonds and then used her escape route to get out of the temple. I saw her sneak into the hall and steal the horn, but what happened then?"

"I snuck back to the temple," Ellette piped up, "threw a stone at Aelwulf to make him chase me, then doubled back and opened the temple door. I helped untie the others and let them out," the little girl paused, clearly pleased with herself.

Hild took up the story, "By the time Aelwulf returned, Raedann was able to jump him and bundled him into the temple before he knew what had hit him."

Anna was impressed, but she was also angry and wanted to know what had happened afterwards. She glared at Lar,

"What then, though? Did you and Raedann agree to sell the horn after all?"

"I hope not," said Gurthrunn. "If you did, child, I am most displeased. The few silver coins you would get would not be worth the chaos the horn could release in the wrong hands."

"Relax both of you. Raedann is not going to sell the horn," Lar answered.

"How can you be so sure? He is a tinker after all. You let him leave with it. What did you think he would do with it?" Anna asked.

"Oh, I have no doubt that once away from the village he would do exactly that. I certainly would," Lar grinned.

"Enough teasing them, Lar," Wilburh said. "We don't have time for this. We need to find a way to escape before they catch him."

"Why?" Gurthrunn asked.

"Because," said Ellette, "when they do catch him they will discover that he does not have the horn, which would be bad for Raedann. And then they will come straight back here, which would be bad for us."

"But I thought you said ..." Anna paused as she realised what Ellette had said. "Why would it be bad for us?"

"Because Raedann does not have the horn, Anna. I do!" The small girl gave a big smile and patted a bulge in her dress. "It's under here."

"So it was a trick. That was clever," Anna smiled back.

"Yes. It worked on you and I figured it would work on the rest of the village. They all know Raedann and what he is like. All we had to do was shout after him not to sell the horn."

Looking from one to another, the dwarf suddenly laughed, "Clever children. That was most ingenious."

"Yes they have their moments," Anna agreed. "But what now? What do we do?"

Lar's grin immediately disappeared. "Well, there we have a problem. We had not anticipated being tied up and locked in here. You see, the idea was for you to use the horn. It is bound to you. It is yours to command. If it really can call up an army it strikes me that this would be a very good time!"

"Use the horn?" Anna echoed doubtfully. "Are you sure we should?"

"We don't, YOU do," Wilburh said.

Anna shook her head. "I ... I don't know. Gurthrunn said it chooses a warrior, a leader of warriors and a champion. I don't feel like any of those any more. What if I can't do it? What if I can't lead as I should? What ... what if the horn chose wrong?"

Then that presence in her head was back and this time the voice spoke out loud so they could all hear it – and it sounded annoyed.

SHIELD MAIDEN

"I choose wrong? The very idea is preposterous! I have been in existence for ten thousand and more years. I have seen wars and battles, heroes and cowards and I tell you that I know a champion when I see one. Doubt no more, child of Midgard. Use my powers and summon an army for you to command."

The voice died away, but Anna could still feel its presence in her mind, waiting for her to make her decision.

Decision – yes, that was what it was all about in the end. For leaders, champions and heroes, there comes a time when they must make the decision to accept what fate has chosen for them no matter what that fate may be. Anna knew in that moment that for her the time had come. She eyed Ellette, who with her back to Gurthrunn and the boys was fumbling with her bound hands beneath her dress. The little girl retrieved the horn and with a triumphant smile held it out. Anna stared at it for a moment, hesitating one last time and then she nodded her head.

The decision now made, she took the horn from Ellette then looked around in the gloom at the expectant faces of her companions. "Very well; I will do it. I will blow the horn. Merciful Woden, watch over us when I do!"

CHAPTER FIFTEEN
ANNA USES THE HORN

"First things first," Hild said, struggling without success to free herself. "How do we get out of these ropes?"

"Yes," said Lar. "I thought you dwarves were strong. Can't you break the rope?" he asked Gurthrunn.

The dwarf shrugged and tried, grunting with effort, but finally shaking his head. "The bonds are too tight around my wrists - I cannot move them."

"What about you Wilburh," Anna asked. "Surely there is a spell to untie knots or burn rope?"

The dark-haired boy shook his head. "I could burn the rope, certainly, but in order to focus the elements I need to move my hands in a certain way as I speak the words."

"So you are saying that in order to get yourself free so you can move your hands, you first must be able to move your hands?" Lar asked drily.

Wilburh nodded.

"Can't you just have a go?"

"Yes, but if I do not get it right I could burn down the hut or set someone alight."

"Ah," Lar's eyes widened. "On second thoughts, let's not do that. Next plan anyone?"

"Do not panic. I have everything under control,"

Ellette said. "They stared at her and saw that she held out her hands in front of her, free of the rope and was wriggling her fingers at them.

"She's done it again!" Hild gasped. "How do you do that?"

"There are advantages to being little you know." Ellette looked smug as she turned away from them and climbed onto a barrel, reaching up for the large broad-bladed seax that hung from a hook on the wall and was normally used to cut meat into joints. Clambering back to the floor, the little girl crossed to Gurthrunn and used the sharp edge to release first him and then the others.

"Look for something to use for weapons," Anna ordered as soon as they were free. They searched the storeroom and found three knives, an axe for chopping wood, a hunting bow, several dozen arrows and a sling.

"Lar is the best shot with the bow so let him have that. Hild can have the sling," Ellette suggested, again looking smug. "I still have my sling. I had it hidden in my pouch and they didn't bother to look." She pulled the small leather weapon out and showed it to them along with a handful of pebbles.

"Agreed," Anna said, "and Gurthrunn would be best with the axe as he is the strongest. That is ..." she turned to the dwarf, "are you all right? Meccus gave you a fearful battering."

Gurthrunn nodded. "Unlike you humans, we dwarves heal very quickly."

"Good. Then I will take the seax. Hild, you and Ellette can have a knife each, you too Lar."

"So we are all armed," Lar said, testing the bowstring and squinting down the length of the arrows before pushing them through his belt. "Well ... armed as best as we are able. What now? Do you blow the horn?"

Anna shook her head. "Not in here. If an army arrives I don't think many will fit in here do you? No, we break the door down and I get outside and then sound the horn and pray to the gods that help comes swiftly. Then we must reach Kendra and get that necklace off her. Without it the villagers will not follow her."

"There are still the svartálfar to contend with and Kendra herself. Valkyries are fearsome warriors," Gurthrunn said. "But your plan is as good as any other I can think of. Remember, though, that once we are through the door, speed is the key. We must reach Kendra before she can recall the villagers, regardless of what help does or does not come when you sound the horn."

Anna nodded.

"Ready then?" Gurthrunn asked, hefting the axe in one hand and gauging its weight.

"Yes ... I suppose so. Break the door down," Anna ordered.

Gurthrunn planted himself in front of the door and balancing his weight evenly on both feet, he swung the axe back and forth a few times. Then he gave one almighty heave. The blade came down and crashed into the timber planks of the storeroom door. The blow smashed the axe head right through it, and as the dwarf pulled back on it a big chunk of wood came away.

"Again!" Anna urged him, but Gurthrunn was already launching another attack. This one brought away a whole plank. The dwarf reached forward and heaved at the next one. After a moment's grunting and puffing, the plank gave way with a loud crack. The hole was now wide enough for the children to squeeze through. Anna led the way, seax in one hand and horn ready in the other. Lar came next and stood beside her as he notched an arrow onto his bow. The others followed, and finally Gurthrunn burst through, sending splinters of wood flying in all directions.

They stood for a moment, listening. It seemed impossible that no one had heard the racket as they smashed their way out, but at first it seemed so, for there was no immediate sign of life in the village.

"That's odd," Lar commented.

"I think Kendra has sent everyone after Raedann," Anna suggested. "I hope he can run fast. I ..." but her voice trailed off because they had all heard a cackle and screech from around the front of the headman's hall. A moment later, several more voices joined in: high-pitched, taunting voices and most definitely not human.

"Svartálfar!" Gurthrunn exclaimed. "Get ready."

As best as they could, they each prepared for the onslaught. Gurthrunn had the small axe in one hand and in the other he held part of a splintered plank of wood. Used as a club it could give someone a nasty blow and might parry blades and spears, a little like a shield. Lar had an arrow aimed at the corner of the hall. Ellette was swinging a stone in her sling. Wilburh was muttering under his breath, his fingers twitching in preparation for some magical spell. Hild had her knife ready, but she and the others knew she was of little use with it. At her waist was her pouch of herbs and healing salves. Anna hoped nobody would need them, but it was good to know that Hild was there if they did. Holding up the seax in one hand, with the other Anna raised the horn to her lips.

"*Not yet,*" the voice sounded in her head.

"But they are coming!"

"*I work best when the foe is upon you.*"

Anna frowned and looked down at the horn. "You are only saying that because you like people to see how powerful you are. You are a show off!"

"*I would not have put it quite that way,*" the horn said, sounding a little hurt.

"Sorry," Anna apologised. But the horn said no more

because at that moment fifty of the svartálfar burst into view around the corner, spotted Gurthrunn and the children and screeching triumphantly, charged towards them.

"*Now!*" the horn shouted.

Anna took a deep breath, brought the horn up to her lips, waited a fraction of a second and then blew.

Just as before, the sound began deep under their feet, rather like distant thunder at first, but then rolling closer and closer until it reached a deafening crescendo, which shook the very buildings around them and vibrated through the iron of the weapons in their hands. The svartálfar halted in the middle of their charge and cried out in terror, falling to their knees and dropping their weapons to clamp their hands tightly around their eyes and ears.

Anna, her ears ringing, felt the horn's regret as the sound died away and silence fell upon them all. For a moment afterwards no one moved. Then one by one the dark elves peeked out from between their fingers, took their hands away from their faces and retrieving their weapons, climbed back onto their feet. The creatures looked at each other with relief then turned to glare with murderous intent at Anna and her friends.

"What happened?" Ellette asked. "Is it broken?"

"Well are you?" Anna asked the horn as she took it away from her mouth and gave it a little shake.

"*Please don't do that! I am not broken. You must have patience.*" the horn answered. "*Give it a short while and an answer will come.*"

In front of them the svartálfar were moving slowly forward, still cautious it seemed. Then one of the dark elves raised his knife in the air, gave out a cry and charged, quickly followed by the others.

"We don't have a short while, horn!" Anna hissed, but the horn did not respond.

"Get ready," Gurthrunn said. "Here they come!"

CHAPTER SIXTEEN
BRISINGAMEN

Snarling and hissing in their rage, the dark elves hurtled towards the children, each of them seemingly trying to outdo the others to reach the humans and dwarf first. Lar released his arrow and it flew straight and true to kill a dark elf. Ellette grunted as she let fly with her sling and a stone clattered into the skull of another svartálfar sending it senseless to the ground. Two down, but twenty-eight more charged onwards. Lar had time for one more shot, which caught an enemy in the arm and knocked the creature back into another, the two elves landing in a tangled heap.

But it was not enough: the enemy was upon them!

The first dark elf darted towards Anna, swinging his short, curved sword like a scythe. She dodged away and stabbed back with her seax. The knife clanged onto the elfin blade and sent the dark elf hopping back to regain his balance. But others quickly replaced him and were reaching for her, snarling their fury as she lashed out with her seax.

Wilburh's hands were moving in a blur and his lips almost as quickly as he conjured a silver bolt of light and hurled it at the elves, not even bothering to see what damage it had done before repeating the incantation. Close by,

Gurthrunn was roaring as he hacked back and forth with the axe, just as if it was the hammer of the thunder god, Thunor, and not something used to chop wood. Each blow that connected meant another dark elf killed or wounded, but still the enemy swarmed around them, rushing in to attack and then jumping away if a child or the dwarf turned against them, only to leave a gap for another dark elf to dash into. Anna slashed out at one, her seax opening a deep wound all down its arm and the creature, howling in outrage and pain, scampered away. But then two others moved in, calling to her in their strange language: laughing and taunting at the same time.

"There are too many of them!" she shouted.

"I know, but we must reach Kendra soon or it will be too late," Gurthrunn yelled back. "You go and see if you can get the necklace off her, Anna. Take your little friend with you. We other four will try to hold these pesky elves."

"We can't leave you!" Anna protested.

"You must. If the villagers return whilst Kendra still holds the Brisingamen and before whatever help the horn has called arrives, then all is lost."

"I suppose you are right. Very well then. Ellette, you come with me," Anna ordered. "Quickly! Kendra will still be in the hall."

They set off at a run back the way they had come, passing the shattered storeroom door from which they had so recently escaped. On the far side of the food store was the rear entrance to the kitchen, so as to allow the cook easy access to the supplies. This led through to the headman's hall. Reaching the kitchen doorway, the two children hesitated as they waited to see if the room was occupied by dark elves. Ellette snuck forward, almost hugging the rear wall of the hall to peer around the back door. Anna held her breath, expecting at any moment that one of those vicious curved blades would stab out at the little girl. But nothing happened and Ellette turned to grin at Anna, who then moved forward, pushing past Ellette into the kitchen.

The cook was usually a tidy woman who kept her tables and cooking area clean and free from clutter. On an ordinary day a fire would always be burning in the hearth and a pot of broth boiling upon it. Nearby there would be dough being kneaded into flatbread, and herbs being prepared to flavour the meat ready for boiling or roasting. Today none of this was happening. The hearth fire was long cold. There was dough on the table, but it was neglected and almost dried out. A pair of uncooked chicken carcases lay abandoned on a nearby platter, flies buzzing round it.

"Looks like even the cook has joined the hunt for Raedann," Ellette whispered. "She is a bit fat and slow though, so I don't think the tinker has much to worry about from her." Anna nodded, raising a finger to her lips to hush her companion's chatter.

They had reached the inner door that led into the main hall and the two girls now paused and exchanged anxious glances before peering into the room beyond. There were no tapers burning and the fire, which had been raging earlier, had been allowed to die down. The room was dark with foreboding. At first it seemed empty, but after her eyes had adapted to the dim red glow given out by the embers, Anna realised someone was there.

The noise of the battle outside: the screeching and cackling of the dark elves; the clang of metal on metal and the screams and cries of the wounded, filtered into the hall. Yet here, safe inside, Kendra sat alone. Anna had to look twice to be sure her eyes were not deceiving her. Seemingly oblivious to the fighting, the Valkyrie was combing her hair whilst gazing at her beautiful face in a silver mirror. The necklace was still at her throat, sparkling with a ruby glow. Outside, the svartálfar were dying for her and yet here she was, worrying more about her appearance than their lives.

Anna moved towards her, so taken aback by the sight that for a moment she did not realise Kendra had seen her reflection in that same mirror, was fixing her with an intense glare and speaking to her.

"You would sneak up behind me whilst I make myself ready to rescue my Lord?"

"I ... I ..., " stammered Anna. She tensed with alarm as

Kendra put down the mirror, rose gracefully to her feet, turned and stepped forward. It seemed the Valkyrie was not making any threatening moves, however. On the contrary, she was smiling as though welcoming a guest.

Anna gaped then glanced across to the doorway, where only a moment ago Ellette had been standing beside her. She was startled to find that the little figure was nowhere to be seen. Had she slipped away or was she somewhere in the hall, hiding in the shadows that filled every corner, preparing to attack Kendra? If so, Anna had to keep the woman talking in order to give Ellette an opportunity to sneak up on her.

"Your Lord? Do you mean Loki? Is he not chained up for betraying the other gods ... at least, so the story goes," Anna added quickly, seeing the smile wiped off Kendra's face to be replaced by a dangerous expression that reminded Anna of the snake in the ruined villa, the way it had looked as it prepared to strike.

"You, little girl, know nothing," Kendra sneered. "Loki is in captivity at present, but not for much longer. The time is approaching when I will lead an army to storm the very gates of Asgard to free him."

"But why?" Anna heard the faintest noise over to the side of the hall. Certain now that Ellette was sneaking around in the darkness, she carried on talking, moving past the Valkyrie to the opposite side of the hall. Kendra turned to follow, never letting her gaze drop.

"Why are you doing this, Kendra?" Anna raised her voice to cover the sound of Ellette's movement, saying anything she could think of to keep the conversation going. "You Valkyries are given great respect by my people. We honour you for being servants of the gods."

Kendra gave a mocking laugh. "Servants of the gods you say? For hundreds of years I have done as they told me to. I have flown to battlefields and taken away the souls of those who got themselves killed in their stupid wars. The Lord Loki has promised me so much more than that. When I have freed him, together we will overthrow the gods and all will bow to us as King and Queen of Asgard."

"But how can he marry you? Is he not already married to the Goddess Sigyn?"

"She is nothing to me! He has promised to put her aside and take me as his wife instead. I will be queen over the gods. Now do you understand why I do all this?"

"And you trust him? The trickster god?" Anna saw a movement in the gloom beyond the Valkyrie. Ellette had sneaked close behind Kendra and was reaching up with a knife. The little girl seized the necklace and in one movement slashed through the cord that held it around Kendra's neck.

The woman shrieked as the Brisingamen tumbled away from her and fell to the floor. Spinning round, she lunged at Ellette, but the small girl scampered away from her, back into the gloom. Anna took her chance and jumped forward, seized the glittering necklace and then rolled out of the way as the Valkyrie, her face a mask of white hot fury, drew a seax from her belt and lashed out at Anna, missing her throat by no more than the width of a hair.

On all fours, Anna scrambled away from Kendra's slashing blade then jumped to her feet. She saw Ellette running for the front door.

"Ellette, catch!" she cried, and tossed the necklace to her.

As the treasure spun through the air, Kendra gave a cry of alarm and leapt up high in a desperate attempt to catch it. But the Brisingamen passed by just inches from her outstretched fingertips. With a shout of triumph, Ellette caught it in mid-air and ran on to the exit. The Valkyrie shot Anna a venomous glare then pursued the little girl outside.

Drawing her seax, Anna followed. As she burst out of the dark hall into the sunlight she saw Ellette sprinting hard towards the battle that was still going on between the dark elves and her friends. She could see that the svartálfar had suffered casualties and that Lar was bleeding from a wound on his arm. Wilburh looked exhausted from repeatedly casting spells, but she could see neither Hild nor Gurthrunn.

Running at full speed on Ellette's heels, Kendra was fast catching up, and now her ravens joined her, leaving their perch on the roof of the hall to fly alongside their mistress. Although Ellette was the swiftest person Anna knew, Kendra was a Valkyrie and whether on horseback or on foot, few except the gods could outrun a Valkyrie. Kendra had soon caught up and stretching out a hand, clamped it down on the little girl's shoulder. Above her, eyes glistening, wicked beaks ready to stab, the ravens circled and screeched.

Ellette yelped in alarm, but did not panic. Holding up the necklace, she shouted at the top of her lungs, "Gurthrunn!"

The dwarven warrior shot out from the middle of a group of svartálfar, saw what was happening and swatting dark elves aside with his axe, reached out with his hand. As Kendra leant forward to snatch the Brisingamen from Ellette's grasp, the small girl threw it with all her might towards Gurthrunn.

"Catch it!" Kendra screamed. The dark elves stopped fighting and turned to see the necklace arcing high above them. A raven swooped at it, but its talons closed on empty air. Eight of the elves leapt high off the ground in a desperate attempt to seize the treasure for their mistress. But one armoured fist reached higher, and with a roar of triumph, Gurthrunn grabbed hold of the Brisingamen.

By now Anna had almost caught up and was just behind

Kendra, who still clasped Ellette by the shoulder whilst screaming at the dark elves, "Stop him!"

Gurthrunn was holding the necklace above his head. Anna could see his lips moving and knew he was speaking words in the dweorgars' language. Suddenly, a bright golden glow illuminated him and the treasure. In that same instant a flash of light shot away from the necklace and flew outwards, crossing the land beyond the village.

"No!" Kendra snarled, "What have you done, dweorgar?"

Gurthrunn glanced across at her and smiled. "I have cancelled the spell you cast, sorceress. The villagers are freed from their slavery to you and even now will be rushing back here, wanting vengeance and justice for what you have done to them and their children."

Kendra stared at him in silence for a moment and then her lips curled into a snarl. "Very well. Then I shall have to be ready for them."

Turning to her ravens she spoke a few words and they flew away up into the sky, circled for a moment and then vanished into thin air. Anna gasped and hearing this Kendra swung round and smiled at her, a smile full of triumph and mockery.

"You think you have won this day? You have won nothing! My servants have gone to Svatalfaheimr: to the land of the dark elves to summon an army of svartálfar. Soon I shall have the horn and the necklace and all will bow before me. Then I will destroy this useless place and everyone in it before I leave to rescue my lord: Lord Loki!"

CHAPTER SEVENTEEN
THE BATTLE OF SCENESTANE

"Well did you hear that? She is sending for her own army. Where is mine eh? When will help come?" Anna silently asked the horn.

"*Patience, mortal child. It is coming,*" was the only response she got.

Whilst Kendra and Anna stared up into the skies where the raven had vanished, Ellette took advantage of the moment to wriggle out of the Valkyrie's grasp and scampering out of her reach, dashed towards where Gurthrunn and the others were still fighting the dark elves. Although more than a dozen svartálfar now lay dead or wounded at their feet, the children were in grave danger. Lar was looking weak from lost blood and Wilburh, himself exhausted by all his use of magic, was now wielding a knife, trying to keep the dark elves away from the older boy whilst Hild bandaged his wound. Gurthrunn was still a threat to the enemy, however, and his axe, which had caused them so much pain, was swinging back and forth.

The svartálfar were keeping back from that axe, but even now they were moving around to the left and right, trying to encircle Anna's friends. Ellette saw this and finding some pebbles and her sling started firing at them again. Kendra spotted what she was doing and took two steps towards her, but then stopped, turned and stared past Anna.

Wondering what Kendra was looking at, Anna heard a shout from behind her and swinging round scanned the big open field south of the village. At first all she saw was the wheat growing tall and golden. Then she saw a figure beyond it, pushing through the same hedges that she and the others had fled through the previous day. 'Merciful Woden,' Anna thought, 'but was it only yesterday?' Squinting into the distance, she recognised her father. Nerian was coming back to his village and he looked angry. In one hand was his sword. With his free hand he beckoned to half-hidden figures in the bushes and soon more villagers were emerging on either side of him. There was Iden the priest and Meccus the blacksmith, still holding his hammer. He must have taken it on the hunt for Raedann ... Raedann? Where was he, Anna wondered? Had the villagers caught and hurt - or worse killed - him before the spell of the necklace had been broken? Thirty villagers were trampling through the wheat now and coming up into the village.

Seeing their approach the surviving dark elves screeched in fear and scampered away from Anna's friends towards Kendra. The sorceress, however, did not run. Neither did she look afraid as Nerian stomped up to her and thrust his sword point close to her chest.

"I would have words with you, deceiver. We welcomed you as a guest into our village; invited you into our hall and you betrayed that hospitality. You cast foul magicks upon us to twist our minds and bend our wills to your own. You will answer for these charges."

Kendra stared back at him and lifted her chin in a gesture that suggested she felt far above him and that it was beneath her even to acknowledge him, never mind reply.

"Well, Kendra, what is your response?"

Again the Valkyrie said nothing, but around her the dark elves, which until a moment before had been hiding and cowering behind her, suddenly grew excited and starting to creep forward, spreading out to face the villagers. Their fear was gone and now they lifted their cruel, curved blades or short spears and waved them threateningly as they advanced.

Anna frowned, wondering what had caused this sudden change in them. Then she noticed that the air, which until now had been still, was moving. At first it was merely a gentle breeze, but soon a strong wind was building up and then, quite suddenly, it seemed as if a gale was blowing through the village. The svartálfar were cackling and screeching in delight whilst the villagers stared up into the skies in fear.

Above Kendra the clouds were moving, racing across

the skies towards each other and merging into one huge, dark mass. Now, fizzing and crackling, the big black cloud spat forth bolts of lightning. One hit the ground near Anna's father with an ear-splitting crack and all around him the ground was black and smoking. Nerian gave a shout of alarm and stepped back. Then his face grew grim and determined as he lifted his sword and advanced upon the Valkyrie.

"You may control the skies, sorceress, but I am Nerian, son of Oswy, warrior of Scenestane and I do not fear you." With that, Nerian charged and encouraged by this the other villagers roared out a battle cry and ran to join him.

Kendra smiled and thrust one fist skyward, whilst the other pointed directly at Nerian. Crack! A bolt of lightning shot straight at her, but it did not hurt her. In fact, to Anna's eyes it seemed to pass straight through her and then shot out of her pointing finger directly at Nerian, striking his sword. There was a flash and a moment later Nerian was lying on the floor, smoke rising from his unmoving body.

"Father!" Anna screamed, running towards him. She never got there because someone had wrapped one huge arm around her. It was Gurthrunn. Next to him, looking on with terror on their faces were the other children. Lar now saw that his father was not moving and with a gasp he too began to run towards him, but Gurthrunn dropped his axe and seized the back of Lar's tunic.

"What are you doing, I must help him," Lar shouted.

"Yes, let us go!" Anna begged, but Gurthrunn was shaking his head.

"Look!" he commanded, nodding towards the sky.

They looked and Anna saw that the ravens were returning. As she watched, they once more homed in on the Valkyrie, flying round her in a wide circle, and beneath them the air all around Kendra seemed to grow hazy and then blurred. A moment ago there had been only the twenty surviving svartálfar standing there. Then, without Anna being aware of the moment they appeared, she could now see fifty! An instant later she blinked because now there were more than a hundred. The next moment they had doubled yet again, and now two hundred dark elves stood around the sorceress, snarling and hissing, their blades sharp and their expressions vicious. Kendra's army had arrived!

The most vicious of all was a huge dark elf. Taller and broader than the rest he was the height of a human man. In his hands was a huge two-handed sword and on his head he wore a crown. The elf king turned and bowed to Kendra and then studied the villagers as if waiting for the word to attack them all.

While the elf army had appeared as if from nowhere, the villagers and the children had looked on in spellbound amazement, frozen by both terror and astonishment to the spot on which they stood. And so they might have remained had the warrior dwarf not stirred himself.

"Run!" Gurthrunn roared.

His order broke the spell upon everyone. The villagers turned to flee back towards the wheat, which was being buffeted by the storm still raging over Kendra's head. Gurthrunn dragged the children up the path leading to the little temple in its glade.

"Kill them all!" screeched Kendra and released by her command the svartálfar leapt into the attack. One hundred elves led by their mighty king charged after the villagers. The other hundred turned to pursue the children up the path.

"Back, get into the temple!" Gurthrunn ordered.

The svartálfar were closer now, scuttling up the muddy path like a swarm of bees chasing someone who had disturbed their nest. One threw a spear, which Gurthrunn swatted aside. A second one caught him in the arm and roaring with the pain he pulled the point out of him and flung the spear back, killing the very elf who had thrown it at him. Then he spotted a large branch lying on the ground and picking it up he turned and advanced down the path into the horde, swinging the branch like a club. Three more elves were knocked down, but there were simply too many of them and Anna knew that all too soon he would surely be overwhelmed.

"Anna," Lar shouted, "we have to do something quickly!"

She nodded her head, but was at a loss about what to suggest. They were all exhausted, wounded and afraid. What could she do?

She could try. At least she could try. She followed the battling dwarf back down the path, seax held in one hand and horn in the other. The dark elves studied her as she moved towards them, their faces sneering and taunting. Then they must have seen something in her expression, for there was no longer any sneering. Instead a grim threat took over their faces. They came towards her, treating her to the same look of wary respect they wore when approaching Gurthrunn. Anna still felt afraid, but she felt something else. She felt like a warrior. Almost without thinking about it she heard herself challenge the enemy in words that sounded just like her father.

"I am Anna, daughter of Nerian, shield maiden of Scenestane and I do not fear you," she said. Then she added. "Fear me instead!"

And lifting the horn again she blew one more time and the svartálfar recoiled at the sound. As the notes died away Anna was aware of a new feeling. There was expectation in the air now. Her call had been answered and something was coming.

"Yes, at last you are my champion and at last it is time," the horn answered her.

"Your army is coming to your call!"

CHAPTER EIGHTEEN
ANNA'S ARMY

One moment Anna was standing alone in the grove between the other children at the temple door and Gurthrunn, who was now surrounded by dark elves. The next second an army had appeared all about her, an army of the warrior women of the gods: an army of Valkyries. Each one was taller than most men in Anna's village and powerfully built, wearing chain armour and bearing fearsome-looking axes or swords, and shields.

'So this is what Kendra once looked like,' thought Anna, as one of the women, with long, almost silvery hair, stepped forward and stared at her.

"I am Lydia, Chieftain of the Valkyries. Who, mortal child, are you that you dare to summon us with that horn?"

"My name is Anna. I do not have time to explain. There are dark elves here," she pointed at the svartálfar that were even now backing away from the new arrivals. "See there. That is not all. One of you, a Valkyrie named Kendra, is their leader."

"Kendra? She is here?"

Anna nodded. "She is after this horn - Heimdall's horn. But I found it and blew it and that is how you are here."

The warrior woman studied Anna for a moment, her

eyes narrowing. "Kendra is our sister," she said at last.

Anna felt her heart sinking. Had she called yet more allies to fight alongside the sorceress? If so there were all doomed.

"She is indeed our sister," Lydia said, "or was, but she betrayed us and the gods. She took service with the trickster god and fled Asgard with other faithless ones and many treasures. She is no longer one of us."

"So, will you help us?" Anna asked.

The Valkyrie bowed her head. "You blew the horn. It only calls for one who it deems a champion. We answer the call. My sisters and I stand ready to go where you lead. We will fight who you fight and strive for your victory. What is your command, champion?"

Anna's legs were trembling with relief and it took her a moment to recover from hearing this powerful warrior woman refer to her as 'champion'. Then she heard villagers screaming, their cries for help carrying up to the grove. She had to act right now. "Follow me, we attack the elves and Kendra and save my people," she shouted, turning to run down the path, her seax at the ready.

The Valkyries followed her and behind them came Lar, Wilburh, Hild and Ellette. Anna reached Gurthrunn, who was struggling back onto his feet. Giving him a quick smile, she took up position at the dwarf warrior's side and then, with an army of Valkyries coming up behind her, Anna led the charge against the dark elves. Taking one look at Anna's army, they turned as one and fled down the hill.

Whooping, Anna chased them, running along the tree-lined path and down to the village where Kendra, with lightning still spitting from her hands and storm clouds swirling over her head, was screaming at the dark elves to turn and fight. Intimidated by the sorceress, they did as she commanded, holding up their weapons and snarling at the approaching enemy.

"Gurthrunn, Lydia: attack Kendra," Anna shouted. "Send some of your sisters with me. My friends and I are going to save our people." Without looking back to see if her command was being obeyed, Anna ran on southwards, heading for the open field beyond the wheat strips where she and her companions had hidden from Iden.

The villagers had fled back towards the woods, but the svartálfar were faster and had cut them off. Now, one hundred of the vicious dark elves had surrounded them and were swarming around, snarling and threatening the thirty adults with their spears and swords. The villagers were mostly farmers and craftsman; few were warriors. Those who were - like Meccus the blacksmith - were swinging blades and hammers or threatening the elves with slings and bows. But they were vastly outnumbered and as the dark elves closed in on them the villagers were doomed.

Or would have been were it not for Anna, who now led her friends and a dozen Valkyrie on a rescue attempt.

"*Heoruflá æledfýr!*" shouted Wilburh, who seemed to have forgotten his exhaustion and got his strength back. His hands shot forth bolts of blazing fire, which incinerated half a dozen elves. Lar, standing tall despite his wound, wielded his bow and without waiting to see if his first arrow had scored a hit, reloaded and sent another one into the enemy. Ellette and Hild were circling off to the left, their slings whirling above their heads, pelting stones at the vile creatures. Then the Valkyries arrived with their swords and Anna with her seax and the hand-to-hand fighting began.

Anna jumped forward to stab at an elf that had been threatening one of the old folk, but she was forced to retreat again as three svartálfar lunged at her, their curved blades cutting through the air where she had been standing just moments before. One of the Valkyries appeared at Anna's side and struck two of these attackers down with her sword and Anna advanced once more.

So the battle raged on, full of movement and fury, back and forth, cut and thrust, stab and parry. Anna's ears rang with the crash of steel on steel, the screaming and shouting of the fighters, the twang of bowstring, the whirring of arrows and whirling of slings, and over it all, the boom of Wilburh's magic.

To begin with, the elves had been taken by surprise by Anna's charge and she and her companions had made headway into the horde of svartálfar that swarmed around the villagers. But the elves quickly recovered and they outnumbered Anna's army two to one: it was eighty elves against forty humans and Valkyries. The fighting now got really tough: two Valkyries were soon killed and a villager also died. Then the dark elf-king's blade cut into Meccus's shoulder and he fell injured to the ground. Without his strong arm to keep them away the elves surged towards the villagers again and two more men were soon badly hurt. Lar had now run out of arrows, Hild's sling had snapped and Wilburh's magic was clearly exhausting him again because he was slumped down on his knees.

Anna stared across the battlefield, her heart sinking. It was clear that the tide was turning and with numbers in their favour the elves would soon overwhelm and kill them all.

"*Now is the moment, champion, the moment when you win the battle,*" the horn's voice sang in her mind.

"What do you mean? What must I do?" Anna asked.

"*That is up to you. Upon a champion's action a battle can turn.*"

"You are a big help!" Anna snapped, her gaze caught by the sight of the dark elf-king, who towered above his warriors. In the midst of the battle, he was spinning round to launch himself at two Valkyries, his huge sword a blur as it whirled around his head. "He is a mighty warrior," Anna murmured under her breath, "he could win the battle for the elves all by himself." Then, suddenly, she knew what she had to do.

The dark elf-king was powerful and mighty indeed, but

Anna had one advantage: she was faster and smaller. She moved around to the left of the pair of Valkyries who were fighting the king. The elf flicked a glance at her, took in her small knife and the fact that she was only a child and dismissed her with hardly even a sneer, turning his gaze back to his enemies.

This was what Anna had hoped for: that the elf warrior would take her as a 'mere girl'. She waited for him to slash at one of the Valkyries and then ran forward, lunging with her blade, not at the body of the elf, protected as it was by his chain armour, but at his arm. With a grunt of effort she stabbed her seax into his forearm, burying it almost to the hilt.

The elven king roared out in pain and dropped his sword. He just had time to glare at Anna with astonishment, before the Valkyries took advantage of his defencelessness to leap in and finish him with their own blades.

As the dark elf-king fell dead at Anna's feet, the effect on the svartálfar army was immediate. They took one look at Anna and the Valkyries standing over their king's body and let out a deep wail. Next, with a clattering noise, their spears and knives fell to the ground. Finally, they turned and ran, scattering in all directions.

In awed silence, for a moment the villagers watched the elves running away and then Meccus, who had dragged himself back onto his feet and was stood cradling his injured arm, started cheering and the villagers all joined in.

Anna lifted her hands to stop the celebrations. "The battle is not over yet," she shouted. "Get back to the village!" With that command she turned to run back towards the headman's hall. Behind her the villagers obeyed her orders without question and followed.

"That was impressive," Lar said, running beside his sister. "What you did there was very brave Anna - very smart, mind you, but very dangerous all the same."

"The horn gave me the idea really."

"*Oh no I did not. That was all your idea. The idea of a champion,*" the horn said to her. Anna looked sideways at Lar to see if he had heard it, for the horn's voice sounded so loud to her, but he seemed not to have done and she concluded that it spoke only into her head, like a thought. "*That's right,*" it said, "*and I can read your thoughts too!*"

Anna had no time to think about this, for now they had reached the village green, only to find that the battle with Kendra's army was all but over. A few clumps of elves were still fighting the Valkyries, but soon these were dead or fleeing. Anna looked around for the sorceress, but could not see her, nor could she spot Gurthrunn. Then she saw that Lydia was kneeling beside Nerian, who still lay motionless on the ground.

"Papa!" she screamed and set off at a run. Her brother overtook her and reached Lydia first, flinging himself to his knees to examine their father.

"Is he...?" Anna asked as Lar bent over Nerian, "... dead?"

Lar leaned closer so that he could hear if their father was breathing. A look of relief came over his face. "He is still breathing, but it is weak. Kendra's lightning bolts must have stunned him, but as far as I can see his wounds are not mortal. He is not dead, Anna, praise the gods!"

Letting out the breath she had been holding, Anna looked around for Hild. She was standing nearby and came running in answer to Anna's beckoning wave. "Hild, look after my father, will you?" The younger girl nodded and before Anna had finished speaking was kneeling over the village leader, studying his wounds.

"Where is Gurthrunn and where is Kendra?" Anna asked Lydia.

The Valkyrie leader hesitated before answering. "My sister struck the dweorgar down and then fled with him before we could catch her."

"That is terrible news," Lar said, getting to his feet.

"Indeed it is terrible," Lydia replied, "but not just for Gurthrunn. He had hold of the Brisingamen, which means she has it now!"

CHAPTER NINETEEN
KENDRA FLEES

"What!" Anna exclaimed. "How? What exactly happened?"

"Kendra might rely on sorcery and devices like the Brisingamen most of the time, but she is still our sister," Lydia said. "As such she is a warrior maiden first and a fearsome one at that. Gurthrunn is a strong warrior too, but a Valkyrie is hard to beat and our strength is much greater than that of a dwarf. She saw the Brisingamen in his belt and attacked him."

"Was he killed?" Ellette asked looking close to tears. "I quite liked him."

"The two of them fought tooth and claw like warrior gods, whilst my sisters and I battled the svartálfar," Lydia explained. "Then, as the battle turned and the elves fled, Kendra seized the Brisingamen and struck Gurthrunn down. Before we could reach them she had whistled for her stallion. It came like lightning to her call and she lifted the dweorgar's body onto its back, mounted up behind him and made off. She is running - even now she is running."

Wilburh frowned. "But if she has the necklace she can enchant more people and force them to do her will. "

Lydia nodded. "Indeed she can."

"Then we must go after her – and quickly," Anna said.

"I can help. We can use my horse," Lydia agreed.

"Your horse?" Anna looked around the village. Here and there pockets of dark elves were still fighting Valkyries. The villagers were slowly returning, the fit and able helping to support the injured. Over in the paddock behind Meccus's smithy Anna could see the two scruffy mares, both looking agitated and leaning over the gate, but nowhere was there any sign of a horse that might belong to a Valkyrie. Lydia saw her puzzlement, smiled and then clicked her fingers.

Anna heard the noise of hoofbeats thundering across turf and gasped. In the blink of an eye, a huge and powerful white stallion had simply appeared next to the Valkyrie, as though it had come out of nowhere. Lydia patted him on the neck and then mounted. Holding out her hand to Anna, she commanded, "Come with me!"

Gulping, Anna just nodded and let herself be pulled up behind Lydia, feeling the animal's back warm and soft against her legs, for the Valkyrie did not use a saddle. "Where are we going?" she asked, trying to speak firmly ... the ground looked an awfully long way away!

"Kendra has ridden north."

"Then I think I know where she is heading." Anna looked down at Lar and the others, "Follow us to the barrow!" she ordered. They gaped up at her, Ellette's face crimson with envy.

"The barrow?" Lar asked with a frown. "Why there?"

"She is using Gurthrunn's route isn't she," Wilburh said. "She is using the barrow to open the Bifrost."

"Ah, so there is a portal to the Bifrost near here? Now I understand. Yes, that is what Kendra will do," Lydia said. "She knows that we her sisters, loyal to the gods as we are, will hunt her down, so she cannot just ride away from your village and hide in the next valley. She will open the Bifrost."

"Is her horse like yours, can it appear and disappear?" Lar asked.

"It is, yes, but we Valkyries could still track her if she chose to stay. She must flee this world of Midgard, for the present anyway. The easiest way for her, given she now has one of the gods' treasures in her possession, is to open the portal. A dweorgar could do that for her. That is why she has taken him, which means he must still be alive."

"Gurthrunn would not do it," said Ellette, springing to the dwarf's defence, her lip thrust out in defiance. "He would not let her get away."

"He may not have any choice, child. Dweorgars built Bifrost and all the other portals to this world. His warm blood alone would open the door given enough power, and with the Brisingamen Kendra has that power.

"Our friend is in mortal danger then?" Anna asked.

"Indeed he is," Lydia nodded. "Enough talk, we ride. Hold tight!" Using only the pressure of her knees, Lydia turned her steed to face north towards the headman's hall. Guiding the stallion with her hands, she nudged it with her heels and the beast leapt forward. Anna gasped, for in an instant they were galloping faster than the wind towards her father's hall.

"The hall!" she shouted out in warning, her hair whipping back from her head.

"Trust me, child!" Lydia answered and clapped her

hand to her steed's neck. Anna felt the stallion's powerful muscles bunch beneath her as it jumped skyward. It was an impossible jump, even for the best of horses and Anna closed her eyes, expecting to feel a gut-wrenching thump as she, Lydia and the horse ploughed into the building. She kept her eyes screwed shut for several seconds, but there was no crash, no impact, just the sensation of ... flying!

She opened one eye and looked down. She could see the beast's legs moving up and down, back and forth as if in full gallop. But beneath the flashing hooves there was just air! They were flying through the air a hundred feet above the trees and brook north of the village.

"Merciful Woden, protect me!" she said. "I have heard stories about Valkyries riding horses through the skies, but I did not believe them."

Lydia turned to shout a reply. "Why should the stories lie? This is what we do. As the gods command it, we ride back and forth between all of the Nine Worlds. How else do you suppose we take the souls of brave warriors to feast with Woden in Valhalla? Ah, now there she is," Lydia pointed.

Anna could see that they were now passing over the ruined villa. Ahead of them was the barrow. She could just make out a figure with a white horse standing near the entrance. Lydia directed her own stallion downwards and it increased speed as they started to descend. As they reached the ground, without breaking stride the horse landed effortlessly and continued to gallop, speeding on across the grassy meadow towards the barrow.

As it drew closer, Anna's eyes widened in astonishment at what she saw: the door of the barrow, which before had been dull stone, was glowing with a bright light. Then she spotted Gurthrunn. The dwarf warrior was slumped down near the doorway. His sleeve was rolled up and she could see it bore a nasty wound. Splatters of blood were splashed around the door frame. They were too late! Kendra had cut him and used his gushing warm blood on the door.

"She is opening the Bifrost. We don't have long," Lydia shouted and urged her mount on even faster.

As they closed upon Kendra, the sorceress turned to glance at them. Irritation showed on her face and she took two steps away from the barrow, held out her hand and a bolt of lightning leapt forth from her fingers and shot towards them.

Lydia spoke a command to her horse. It swerved instantly to one side and the bolt flew past to smash into a tree in the woods behind them. Another bolt came at them and this time Lydia held up her hand, which now glowed with a faint golden light. The lightning bolt hit her palm and deflected away from her.

"How did you do that?" Anna gulped, clinging to the Valkyrie's waist.

"We all have some magic," explained Lydia, "but Kendra was always the strongest of us." As she spoke she slowed the horse to a canter and then stopped. She slid off its back, landing on her feet and drawing her sword in one easy motion. Anna followed suit, hanging onto the stallion's rump so as not to fall. As soon as she felt the ground beneath her feet, she pulled out her seax. They both faced Kendra, who was now barely twenty paces away.

"That I am," sneered Kendra, "much the strongest and yet still you dare to face me?"

"Strongest at magic, I should have said. I was always better with my blade," Lydia said as she moved towards her sister, sword point rising menacingly.

"Why do we need to fight? Why do you two come at me like this? You could join me. Imagine what we three could do together with the Brisingamen and the horn." Her voice was soft and enchanting and Anna might have believed her had she not already seen through Kendra's trickery. She shook her head, but it was Lydia who answered.

"You know that the Brisingamen will not work on me, sister." Lydia glanced at Anna and a smile came to her face, "And it seems not on this mortal child either. We are both too strong for that; too strong for you in fact. Give yourself up and I will speak to Woden and the others and ask them to forgive you."

The sorceress laughed and it was not a nice laugh. "You

would speak to the gods? Do you think they would listen? I betrayed them. Do you think they would be merciful to me? I will not beg for forgiveness."

Lydia moved towards Kendra, sword help at her side. "Can't you see it is over, sister? Give yourself up and your life may be spared."

Kendra shook her head. "You are wrong, sister, it is not over. It has only just begun. You think you have won today. This ... this defeat is nothing. I have lost the horn, but with the Brisingamen and the dweorgar's blood I have opened the Bifrost once more. Everywhere - do you understand me - EVERYWHERE! On all the Nine Worlds, Loki, my master, has followers. The gods thought they had defeated us by closing the Bifrost - but no longer."

"What have you done, Kendra? Do you realise what might happen if the doors between the worlds are open? See what carnage a few svartálfar brought here today. They and a few other beings are the only ones who can travel between the worlds, but if the walls are down and all creatures everywhere can travel as they wish, we could be plunged into chaos again."

Kendra stepped back towards the doorway and smiled. "My master likes chaos," she said. Then the smile vanished as a fist seized hold of the necklace in her hand. Gurthrunn had revived and though he looked weak and very pale and his arm was still bleeding, he had a strong grip on the Brisingamen.

"Your master will not have this!" he hissed at her.

Gasping in shock, Kendra raised her sword ready to stab the dwarf. Lydia leapt forward and blocked the thrust with her blade, but her own sword was knocked out of her hand. The sorceress swung again and in desperation Anna flung her seax. The knife spun over and over and crashed into Kendra's sword, sending it hurtling against the side of the barrow. Now it was the sorceress who was defenceless. She snarled at Anna; took a step towards her, lightning crackling around her right hand. Her left hand still held tightly to the Brisingamen and she and Gurthrunn fought for its possession.

Lydia had retrieved her sword and advanced once more on her sister. Seeing her approach, Kendra let out a great cry of frustration. Releasing the necklace, she jumped through the doorway and ... was gone.

CHAPTER TWENTY
ASGARD

The doorway still glowed and shimmered.

"It is still open?" Anna said. "We could follow her."

Gurthrunn shook his head. "No, we cannot. She could be anywhere. Didn't you hear what she said? She opened all the doors. Bifrost is now linking every world to every other. She could be anywhere in any of the Nine Worlds."

"She has got away then?"

"She has, for now at any rate. But she has not taken the horn or the necklace." Gurthrunn answered, lifting up the Brisingamen. "These at least we denied her. Your village and people are safe, for the moment."

Anna looked around for Kendra's horse, but it too had vanished. She turned back to the doorway, "What do we do about that?" she asked, pointing at the barrow.

"We must certainly take action." Trying to pull himself to his feet, Gurthrunn groaned.

"Sit back down, you are wounded," Lydia knelt beside the dwarf. "The cut on your arm is deep, it needs stitching and binding," she said, examining and probing his wound.

"Ouch!" he muttered, then pointed over the Valkyrie's head and across the field. "Ah, see? Your companions are coming to join us, Anna. They have the tinker with them."

Anna looked towards the village and saw that her brother, their three friends and Raedann were hastening towards the barrow. Seeing Gurthrunn, Hild ran forward, took one look at him, tutted, and rummaging for a needle and thread in the pouch of medicaments that always hung from her belt, she bent to attend to his injuries.

"What happened to you?" Anna asked Raedann whilst Hild worked on the dwarf.

The story teller winked at her. "Well, I led your village folk a merry chase across the fields and woods. Ended up hiding in that cave beneath Grove Hill. I was peeping out to see how close they were when all of a sudden there was this great flash of light and then they all turned away and started running back towards the village. I figured that the spell had been broken and they were on their way to pick a fight with Kendra. Gather from what Lar tells me that it was a bigger fight than I expected. Svartálfar and Valkyries eh? What a story! I will get the details of that tale off you if I may."

Anna grinned, "In a bit, but first we have to decide what to do now. Kendra has gone, but she left the door open. Gurthrunn says we have to take action."

Coming up behind Raedann, Wilburh, still out of breath, was gazing in awe at the shimmering portal. "What is that? he squeaked, pushing past them and pointing at the barrow.

"A gateway to everywhere. It is the Bifrost," Anna said.

"Amazing!" he said, his voice shaking with reverence.

"That's as may be, but it is very dangerous," Gurthrunn said. "We must inform the gods. Anna, you and I must go to Asgard."

Anna's mouth dropped open. "Who, me?"

"Yes you. You are the keeper of the horn. Heimdall will want it back, but only you can carry it to him."

Struggling to his feet, the dwarf smiled at Hild, who had finished binding his arm and salving his various cuts and bruises. "Thank you, child, that feels much better," he said, rolling down his sleeve. "You have the gift of healing and if I'm not mistaken will soon be a famous wisewoman."

Hild blushed, but Gurthrunn had turned his attention back to Anna. "Come child. Follow me," he instructed, walking towards the barrow door.

Lar stepped forward, "I should go with my sister," he said, defiance in his gaze as he eyed the dwarf.

"I am afraid that is not possible," Gurthrunn said. "Although the Bifrost is open, only the gods, beings like Valkyries and us dweorgs as well as those in possesion of the god's treasures may travel to Asgard. Anna is the one who was chosen by the horn and only she may pass through the portal into Asgard. Rest assured that I will do all in my power to protect her in your stead."

Holding the dwarf's gaze for a moment, Lar gave a

reluctant nod and stood back to watch. "We will be here waiting for you, Anna," he called.

She turned to smile at him then followed Gurthrunn. "How do you know the way? How can you be sure we will end up in Asgard?"

The dwarf chuckled. "Anna, we built the Bifrost just as we built all the doors and all the treasures of the gods. I know what I am doing." He held out his hand.

Anna hesitated a moment and then put hers into it. She let herself be led towards the doorway and then closed her eyes as they passed through it. "Tell me when we get there," she said, her eyes still screwed shut.

"We are already there," came his slightly amused reply.

She opened her eyes and stared at him. "But I did not feel anything!"

"Nonetheless, here we are, look." He gave a wave of his hand.

"Merciful Woden!" Anna exclaimed, looking up and around her. They were standing on a triangular ledge on the other side of the doorway, which stood by itself without any walls around it, still shimmering and glowing just as it had in the barrow. Other than themselves and the door, the ledge was empty. On two sides the ground dropped away into an impossibly high cliff. Far below them Anna could see green fields and woodlands stretching into the distance. Behind her, on the third side of the ledge, was a city. She caught her breath in awe. The buildings were like none she had ever seen, built of honey-coloured stone and soaring above them, climbing higher and higher. There were at least a hundred towers, topped by tall spires or minarets, and far above them flags and banners flapped in the breeze. A single, very tall door led from the ledge into the city.

"Well this is pretty scary," Anna whispered to Gurthrunn, staring up at the city in astonishment. "I am thinking of blowing Heimdall's horn again and summoning an army for protection."

"Who is this mortal child who uses my name?" boomed a loud voice. The door into Asgard swung open and Anna gaped in astonishment. The voice belonged to a huge figure that she would hesitate to say was a man, for he was seven foot tall if he was an inch. His skin was the palest white and his hair the fairest blond she had ever seen. He wore a mail shirt that shone and glittered and over which was thrown a dark blue cloak, trimmed with gold. At his side was a mighty sword. He strode onto the ledge and with a piercing gaze peered down at the child and the dwarf.

"Well? Have you no voice, daughter of Midgard? What is this about my horn?"

Anna could not help but recoil in fear, backing away towards the door to the Bifrost. "You heard me say that? But I just whispered it!"

"You will find my hearing is very good, as is my eyesight and both tell me that you have not answered my question: who are you?"

"I ... I am a girl called Anna, and I ... I ..."

"Do you ever get to the point, girl called Anna?" The booming voice echoed about them as if they were in a cavern.

"Yes ... er, Lord Heimdall is it?"

The enormous figure inclined his head, "Yes, I am the God Heimdall, Guardian of Asgard."

"Well then, I have brought you your horn back," Anna said, pulling the treasure from her pouch and lifting it up to him.

Heimdall seemed stunned by the news. He strode forward and bending over her, snatched the horn from her grasp. It looked impossibly small in his great hands, but as he stared at it the horn grew in size to match his stature. Then his gaze snapped back to Anna.

"This has been lost for six of your mortal lifetimes. How did it come to you and how was it you were able to use it?"

"How do you know I used it?" Anna asked.

"It is my horn; I owned it for millennia before it was stolen. Naturally I would know. We heard the call even here in Asgard and dispatched the Valkyries to locate it."

"I will tell the tale, mighty Heimdall," Gurthrunn answered. "But first, may I beg to seek an audience with the Goddess Freya and the God Woden?" As he said this, the dwarf produced the Brisingamen from his belt and held it out. Heimdall took one look at the glittering necklace and nodded his head.

In what seemed like only moments, Anna and Gurthrunn were swept from the entrance into Asgard and led by Heimdall through streets of such splendour that Anna could hardly take it in. She had heard tales of the mighty cities of far away Rome and Byzantium, which were rumoured to be extraordinary, but never in her wildest dreams could she have imagined anything like this and she was both entranced and overawed by the magnificence she saw all around her.

Finally, they were presented in a hall of immense size, with pillars that reached up to a vast dome high above. At the far end of the hall were steps leading up to a dais. There, seated on a vast, stone throne was a being who was both terrifying and wonderful to look at: a mighty warrior, clad in gleaming armour. He had a long, grey-white beard and wore a single eye patch. On the back of his throne were perched two gigantic ravens, and at his feet a pair of wolves regarded their approach with interest. 'Just as a wolf in Midgard might study a herd of deer,' thought Anna, eyeing them warily and feeling very scared. This could be none other than the father of the gods, mighty Woden!

To one side of the throne, a few steps below Woden, two women stood. The first, Anna saw with a start, was the Valkyrie, Lydia, returned it seemed from Midgard. The other was a figure of such remarkable beauty that she took Anna's breath away. She wore a simple, silver coronet atop blonde hair that fell rippling to her waist. Her gown of silver and white shimmered as she moved; her skin was flawless and her smile filled with such sweetness that Anna could not help but smile in return. This, she deduced, was the Goddess Freya.

Gurthrunn bowed and then stepped forward and reached up to hand Freya the Brisingamen. Her expression when she saw it was one of love and affection and it seemed as if a tear came to her eyes as she bent to receive it.

Woden waited until Freya had fastened the necklace around her neck before he spoke. His voice was deep, less booming than Heimdall's, but carrying more authority, as was fitting for the chief of the gods.

"Gurthrunn the dweorgar and a human girl, come together bearing mighty gifts. Well, well: an unusual day indeed. But Heimdall here tells me you have a tale to tell. Let us hear it."

CHAPTER TWENTY-ONE
SHIELD MAIDEN

A nd so they told the tale of how the horn had been found and how Anna had blown it and it had seemed to come to life. How that had brought not just Barghests, but Gurthrunn and finally, Kendra, to their village. Anna explained how she and her friends had sought out Gurthrunn and with his guidance had planned to return the horn to Asgard, only to be ambushed by Kendra. Then Anna described how she had used the horn to summon an army, and told of the battle between the svartálfar and Valkyries. All this was confirmed by Gurthrunn and Lydia, who chipped in from time to time.

Woden listened to the tale and after it had finished he said nothing for such a long time that Anna wondered if he was angry. Had she been wrong to blow the horn? Was she about to be punished? Her legs began to tremble.

"So," Woden began at last, "much has transpired these last few days on mortal Earth. Some good and some ... not so good. The Valkyrie, Kendra, who betrayed us is out there in the Nine Worlds somewhere, plotting and trying to locate the lost treasures of the gods, also trying to raise an army to challenge us and free Loki. The Bifrost has been reopened and Heimdall tells me cannot easily be closed again. The roads and paths between the worlds are unlocked and that can only cause chaos."

"Yet all is not bad. You have retrieved two of the lost treasures and returned them to us so that when war comes to the heavens, as it must, we will have some defence. Kendra's plan failed because of your actions and that is good. Doubly so: good that she failed, although she got away, but especially good because out of this has been born a fresh hope, for Midgard has a new champion in you, mortal child."

"Me?" Anna said meekly.

"*Of course you,*" the horn said in her head.

"Of course you," Woden echoed. "You have returned our treasures and I would not send you home without a reward to help you in the struggles that surely lie ahead."

'Struggles?' thought Anna, 'I don't like the sound of that.'

"*You will be fine, my sister will be with you,*" the horn replied.

'Your sister?' Anna asked in her head, but the horn did not answer this time.

"So, mortal child, I give you this sword, the weapon of a Valkyrie," Woden was saying, showing no indication that he or anyone else had heard Anna's exchange with the horn, except for Heimdall, who was gazing down at her, a flicker of amusement in his eyes.

When Woden stood, Anna saw that he was even taller than Heimdall. He came down from his throne with a sword in his hand and offered it to Anna. Taking it from the god's huge hand she gasped with joy, for it was a blade of great beauty. As her fingers wrapped around the hilt, the sword seemed to alter its size and balance ever so slightly so that after a moment it felt just right for her. At the same time, a strange, tingling sensation passed down her arm and then a voice spoke in her head, but it was not the sing-song, masculine voice of the horn. This was a strong voice too, but it was feminine.

"*Chosen!*" it said, and this time Anna knew what it meant, for she now felt that this had always been her sword. The weapon belonged to her and to no one else. Yes, it was her blade and together they would do mighty deeds.

"*Yes we will,*" the sword answered her thought. "*I am the horn's sister and my name is Aefre - which means 'forever' - for I will protect you as long as you live.*"

Woden gazed down at Anna and almost, he seemed to smile. "The blade of a Valkyrie has never before been given to a child of your world. But you are now Midgard's champion, so wield it well. I will send Gurthrunn back with you. His people know much of what has happened in the past and he can advise you on what might happen in the future. Indeed, I am sure he already knows of the dangers that will surely come."

Gurthrunn bowed, but made no reply.

"How like a dweorgar," Woden said. "Your race says little until it is needed. Very well. Go now, both of you and may your fate - your wyrd - watch over you."

Escorted by Heimdall, they retraced their steps through Asgard until they reached the ledge, where the Bifrost still glowed and shimmered.

"Goodbye, Anna," said the horn from Heimdall's belt.

Heimdall put his hand on it and smiled, "Yes, goodbye, Anna," he said.

She returned his smile and watched as he gave a small bow then went back through the door and closed it behind him.

Going back through the Bifrost, clutching Gurthrunn's good arm in one hand and her new sword in the other, Anna once again kept her eyes shut. When she opened them she was relieved to see that Raedann, her brother and their friends were still there waiting for her at the barrow door.

Right from the start they were stunned by her new sword and all of them, but Raedann in particular, pressed her and Gurthrunn for every detail they could recall of Asgard and the gods. As they strolled back towards Scenestane Anna tried, but found it almost impossible to describe, for there was nothing like it in Midgard to relate it to and she did not feel she could do justice to what she had seen. Even so, the others hung on her words and little Ellette's face was a picture of awe and envy.

"The gods were just like in Raedann's stories, although perhaps even more impressive," Anna finished her tale. "You were even right about Woden only having one eye, Raedann."

"Of course I am right. But have I told you why he has one eye?" the tinker asked.

The children shook their heads.

"Ah," he replied, "thereby hangs a tale, but I'll cut it short. Woden wanted to be wiser than all the other gods, and so he visited the Well of Mimir, who is the wisest being known to the Nine Worlds and lives beneath Yggdrasil, the world tree. Mimir agreed to pass on his wisdom, but demanded Woden's eye in exchange."

"That's dreadful!" Anna shuddered, "I hope I never have to visit Mimir, I don't fancy losing a part of me!"

She was still thinking about it when they reached Scenestane to find the village folk all gathered in Nerian's hall. Anna and Lar were delighted to see their father in his high-backed chair, awake and alert and apparently none the worse for his experience, although his hair was frazzled and there was a faint whiff of smoke coming from his tunic. It seemed that the lightning bolt had melted his sword, but the weapon had deflected the worst of the blast and he had been knocked out, but was otherwise unhurt.

The appearance of Gurthrunn in their village made many of the villagers very nervous, for they had not yet recovered from their battle with the dark elves, the bodies of which still littered the ground outside. Nerian and all the other adults had recalled the arrival of Kendra, but then almost at once they had fallen under her spell and what happened next was hazy. However, between them they had pieced it together and now were horrified as they remembered everything they had done, how cruel they were to the children and how misused they had been by the sorceress.

Meccus begged Gurthrunn's forgiveness for the beating he had given him, then holding Ellette close, his eyes filled with tears and he kept apologising to her.

"It is all right, Father, I am fine," she protested, trying to wriggle out of his embrace. "It wasn't your fault."

Iden was particularly distraught at almost destroying the sacred writings and thanked Wilburh over and over again for saving them. He had been overjoyed, he said, when he got back to the temple to find the scrolls intact and well cared for where Wilburh had placed them.

Nerian also apologised, particularly to Anna, but like Ellette, she brushed it away. "You were not yourself, Papa, there is nothing to forgive." Thanking her, he now pressed the children for the full story of what had happened and so

Anna had to repeat it all over again, including the events of the visit to Asgard.

As she came to the end, Gurthrunn at last spoke. "Anna and her friends have acted beyond their years and shown many talents and abilities. It is because of them that the village survives, but the threat is not over."

"What do you mean?" Nerian asked.

"This land, Mercia - the very word means 'the land on the border', but when your ancestors named it so, they meant a border between the Saxons and the Welsh - now, however, it is truly the land on the border for the Bifrost is opened. The paths between all the Nine Worlds are available for any creature that would tread them. Your village is near those paths. You will need to be alert and cautious and you must be prepared for the dangers to come."

The listening villagers gasped in alarm, but Nerian nodded and thanking the dwarf for his warning, turned to the children. "We have much to thank each of you for and it seems we may have to rely on your help again before long, although next time I hope you will not be quite so much on your own."

He then stood up and moved towards Anna. "As for you, daughter: it appears that I may have been hasty in my decision of a few days ago."

"What do you mean, father?"

"I mean that I have changed my mind. I was mindful of our traditions, as was Iden, when I refused to let you train as a warrior. These past few days suggest that we were wrong. Moreover, if the gods have decreed that you are our champion and Woden has given you that magnificent sword, then who am I to argue?"

"Do you mean ..."

Nerian smiled down at her and nodded.

"Yes, Anna. You may train as a warrior. You will be our shield maiden."

THE END

ABOUT THE WORLD OF SHIELD MAIDEN

Shield Maiden is set in our world in about the year AD 600. These are the years when thousands of Anglo-Saxons are crossing from Germany and Denmark and pushing west, creating a land that will one day be called England.

Anna's people are Angles. Tradition says that the Angles who came to Mercia crossed the North Sea in around 527 and so by Anna's time her people would have lived in Scenestane for over 70 years.

Scenestane itself and the surrounding lands are based on the village of Shenstone. Two Roman roads do cross northwest of the village near the village of Wall - itself the ruins of the old Roman town of Letocetum. Now owned and run by the National Trust, it can be visited, as can the museum there *(www.nationaltrust.org.uk/letocetum-roman-baths/how-to-get-here)*. Evidence of several Roman Villas have been found around the village in archaeological digs over the last century. Likewise there was a barrow north of the village, and on the hills to the west, there is an Iron Age hill fort on private land. Shenstone means 'beautiful stones' and refers to the Roman ruins that would have been visible when Anna's ancestors came to the village. The modern day parish church and the ruins of a much older one are on a rocky hill populated with trees. The English often built their churches on former pagan temples so to me it seemed a good place for Iden's temple.

The Angles were not Christians. Mercian kings allowed Christian missionaries in from AD 633 onwards but it would take a century for it to all become Christian. So Anna, her ancestors and even her own children (if she lives to have them) would be pagan.

ABOUT the GODS

The Anglo -Saxons believed in many gods and goddesses. There are at least fifty different gods, each having care and power over certain aspects of the universe. Anglo-Saxon gods are not always kind. They can be harsh, arrogant and certainly strong-willed. In Shield Maiden we hear about four gods: Thunor is the thunder god. The Vikings called him Thor and that name is more familiar to us today.

Anna actually meets three other gods in person. Here is a little bit about them:

Woden

Name: Woden (Called Odin by the Vikings and Woden in England)

Position: Chief of the gods. God of wisdom and thought. Also a war god.

Appearance: An old man with a long beard. Has only one eye so wears a patch.

Special powers: Can make the dead speak and change men's fate and destiny - their wyrd.

Items of power: The spear Gungnir, which never misses its target. The ring Draupnir, which can make other rings to give as gifts. The eight-footed horse Sleipnir which can ride fast through all the Nine Worlds.

Animal Companion: Woden has two Ravens Huginn and Munin (Thought and Memory)who fly across Midgard to tell him what is happening. He also has two wolves, Freki and Geri.

Notes: It is said that half of those who die in battle are taken to feast with Woden until the end of time in the halls of Vallhalla. Wednesday is named after him as are many villages and towns such as Wednesbury.

Heimdall

Name: Heimdall

Position: Gatekeeper of the gods. Watches the Bifrost - the gateway to Asgard.

Appearance: A handsome young man with blond hair.

Special powers: Has very good eyesight and hearing. It is said that he can hear and see a single blade of grass grow.

Items of power: The Gjallahorn - a horn which can change shape and size and can be used to summon help or an army. Also has a powerful sword.

Animal Companion: None known.

Notes: Heimdall watches the bridge between the worlds. At the end of time he will blow his horn to summon all the gods to war in the final battle of Ragnarok.

Freya

Name: Freya

Position: Goddess of Love and Beauty but also in charge of the Valkyries. Half those who die in battle are sent to her afterlife fields to live with her.

Appearance: very beautiful young woman with long blonde hair.

Special powers: She is a Vanir goddess. The Vanir possessed powerful magic and enchantments.

Items of power: The Brisingamen - a necklace that can control people's minds.

Animal Companion: A cat or pair of cats.

Notes: The constellation Orion in the night sky was once called Freya's belt.

ABOUT The NINE WORLDS

The Anglo-Saxons believed that the universe was a big tree called Yggdrasil. In its branches nine worlds (sometimes seven) were supported. The nine worlds are:

<u>Asgard</u> - home of the gods and location of Valhalla where the dead go to feast with Woden.

<u>Midgard</u> - Our world, Earth. Home to humans.

<u>Vanaheimr</u> - Home to Vanir, gods of magic.

<u>Ālfheimr</u> - The world from which the beautiful light elves come.

<u>Jotunheimr</u> - Land of mountains and giants.

<u>Muspellsheimr</u> - Land of fire and beings of fire.

<u>Svartálfaheimr</u> - Land of the svartálfar dark elves.

<u>Nidarvelir</u> - Land of the dweorgar or dwarves.

<u>Niflheimr</u> - Land of Ice.

In addition, near Niflheimr is Hel (spelt with one l)- the realm of the dead.

This symbol -used by Woden - symbolises The Nine Worlds as three triangles. (It also means Wyrd/fate)

MYTHS AND MONSTERS

The Anglo-Saxons believed in many different creatures and monsters. Anna has encountered these non - human creatures in Shield Maiden

Name: **Barghests** (sometimes called black dogs)
Nature: Huge black dogs or hounds, as large as a calf.
Special powers: They can move silently at times, some can shape-shift.

Notes: These terrifying dogs are often linked to certain roads, gates or locations near water such as a ford or bridge.

Name: **Dweorgar** (dwarves)
Nature: usually described as ugly, often bad tempered and occasionally evil.
Special powers: Dwarves are talented at mining precious metals as well as making magical items and artefacts.
Notes: It was believed that the dwarves invented Runes and writing.

Name: **Svartálfar** (dark elves)

Nature: Very different from the beautiful light elves. Dark elves are often described as ugly and mis-shapen.

Special powers: Can influence human dreams and give nightmares.

Notes: Live underground. Possibly sunlight can turn them to stone.

Name: **Valkyries**

Nature: Immortal angel-like beings in the form of beautiful warrior women.

Special powers: Can fly between the worlds and ride the skies.

Notes: The Valkyries some-times choose who live and die in battle. They also carry the bodies of those slain in battle to the halls of Woden or the fields of Freya.

Name: **Ravens**

Nature: Big black birds.

Special powers: Sharp eyed, these creatures are used as scouts by Valkyries. Woden also owns two Ravens who fly over Midgard and report back to him.

Notes: It was believed that Ravens were bad omens and seeing one meant someone would die.

These were just a few of the creatures who the Anglo-Saxons believed inhabited the woods and hills. It was for fear of them that they avoided such places in the night. When bad things happened they would blame them and they would pray to Woden and Freya to protect their families.

WILBURH'S SPELLS

Wilburh uses a combination of a rune stick (a stick with spells engarved in runes on it), a charm (a collection of twigs and plants tied together) and words to cast his spells. Here are what those spells mean:

Déor áflíeh means "animal flee". Wilburgh uses it to cause the snake to retreat.

Fulbeorht means "full bright or very bright." This is the spell Wilburgh uses to get the torches to flare up brighly.

Heoruflá æledfýr means "arrow +flame of fire" and is used by Wilburgh to shoot a fire bolt at the dark elves.

Sunne- āblænden means "sun+blind" - a blinding spell.

LANGUAGE

Anna and her friends along with all the Anglo Saxons used a language called Old English which evolved out of Old German – the language spoken in the homelands in West Germany. Old English was in use between the 5th and 11th centuries when it merged with Norman French and produced middle English. Modern English came later still.

Old English looks and sounds VERY alien to a modern English speaker. Here is the Lord's Prayer in Old English:

Fæder ure þu þe eart on heofonum; Si þin nama gehalgod
to becume þin rice gewurþe ðin willa
on eorðan swa swa on heofonum.
urne gedæghwamlican hlaf syle us todæg
and forgyf us ure gyltas
swa swa we forgyfað urum gyltendum
and ne gelæd þu us on costnunge
ac alys us of yfele soþlice

Translation of Old English

Father our thou that art in heavens; be thy name hallowed
come thy kingdom; be-done thy will
on earth as in heavens

our daily bread give us today
and forgive us our sins
as we forgive those-who-have-sinned-against-us
and not lead thou us into temptation
but deliver us from evil. truly

RUNES AND WRITING

The Anglo-Saxons originally wrote in an old style using runes. Just as the Welsh alphabet of today has no 'k' and some letters are combined to give different sounds (the tongue-twisting 'll' for example) so too the runic alphabet has some letters missing and some combined. Try writing your name in Runic. For 'c' use the runic character for s or k. For 'q' use k together with w; for 'x' use k and s, and for 'y' use i.

Confused? Well here is an example. My name is Richard. In the Runic Alphabet I would spell it RI<NFRH

Give it a go.

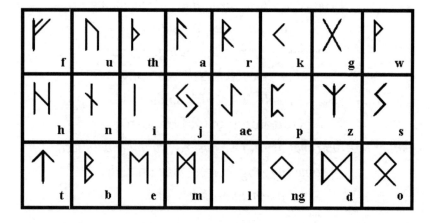

Lightning Source UK Ltd.
Milton Keynes UK
UKOW040653080612

194075UK00001B/1/P